Dedication

To my parents, William and Mary Vogt, and my grandparents,
Peter and Ruth Ruocco, who taught me that anything is possible.

PREVENTIVE OFFICIATING

www.PreventiveOfficiating.com

For questions, comments or suggestions, please contact author Randy Vogt at rvogt1 @verizon.net

ISBN: 1450567622
Printed in the United States of America

Preventive Officiating

How a Referee Avoids
Trouble on the Soccer Field

by Randy Vogt

Acknowledgements

The author would like to thank the following people whose help was extremely valuable in creating this book:

Esteemed soccer journalists **Paul Gardner** and **Michael Lewis** plus authors **John Carinci**, **Father Roland Faley** and **Fred von Burg** for their exemplary guidance

John Sengelaub, whose knowledge of the rules and ability to find the right word were irreplaceable, and **Cathy Cotten**, who volunteered her expertise to professionally edit this book, improving it tremendously

Our models, **David Allen**, **Cathy Caldwell** and **Justyne Passarelli**, who spent a sunny Saturday demonstrating referee and assistant referee signals

Mike Clarke, **Gene O'Connell** and the **Long Island Junior Soccer League** for the use of the Peter Collins Soccer Park

Larry Harris and **Paul Harris**, whose book, Fair or Foul?, gave the author ideas that he still uses today, more than three decades after reading the book. The author is very happy that this book is helping a new generation of referees.

The author would like to also thank all those who have helped him—referees, coaches, players and spectators—during his officiating career.

About the Author

There are 17 rules, or Laws, in soccer. It is imperative that a referee knows all the Laws of the Game to avoid trouble. But as a referee gains experience, he or she utilizes common sense, known as Law 18, to stay out of trouble as well.

Randy Vogt has followed this path during his officiating career. He has officiated over 9,000 games during the past four decades, from professional matches in front of thousands to six-year-olds being cheered on by very enthusiastic parents. Randy has received many officiating awards, has been invited to referee tournaments around the world and refereed in a couple of the globe's great soccer stadiums. In <u>Preventive Officiating</u>, he shares his wisdom gleaned from thousands of games and hundreds of clinics to help referees not only survive but thrive on the soccer field.

Introduction

The purpose of preventive medicine is to avoid health problems before they begin.

Generally, people who eat a balanced diet, watch their weight, exercise, sleep well, keep a positive mental attitude and do not smoke are much healthier than those who do the opposite. It is much less costly, both financially and emotionally, to prevent health problems than to cure them.

Through my four decades of officiating soccer games, I have seen many problems on soccer fields that could have been avoided. If only this official had a better understanding of the rules and how they apply to the division and skill level being played. Or that official had actually run up and down the field or had a better attitude toward the game and its players.

Preventive Officiating will help with many of the challenges facing a new referee or relatively new ref before problems begin. This book was written to help soccer referees with 10 years of experience and under, although officials with all levels of expertise will learn something. It will also provide a greater understanding of the game to help prevent players from becoming injured in some cases. Because, just as in medicine, it's much easier to prevent problems than it is to search for a cure.

-Randy Vogt

Every Beginner Is a Winner

After all, the ark was built by amateurs and the Titanic was built by professionals. You, as a new referee or relatively new ref with several years of experience, have not made anywhere near the number of mistakes that I've made. It is my hope that this book will help you avoid most of them and will help guide you to a fruitful officiating career.

Preparation

You have been assigned three games this Saturday and two on Sunday.

The referee who physically trains for these games and watches officials during other soccer matches will most likely be a good deal more successful than the person who does not think about these assignments all week until putting on a referee uniform that weekend.

Many new referees are surprised at the commitment needed to become a successful official. As I like to say, based on Galatians 6:7, "You reap what you sow."

Training

If you believe that refereeing one or two days per week will make you fit without physically training for it, you are sadly mistaken. Soccer is played at its own pace— some games are fast, others are slow-moving. With relatively unskilled players, there is even some acceleration of play in spurts. Games will be played at a given pace whether the officials can keep up with play or not.

Those officials who do not move up or down the field are the first to complain about overly enthusiastic spectators and often quickly determine that refereeing is not for them. If you are properly prepared for the physical demands of soccer, you will enjoy it much more.

If you have led a sedentary lifestyle, please get the approval of your doctor before becoming a soccer referee and taking on all the physical training that goes with it. The *fartlet* training method works best for me, as it mimics a soccer game. Rather than just jogging, you jog, sprint, jog...with an all-out sprint at the end. If you are currently out of shape, start slowly after getting your doctor's approval and gradually work up to a mile.

As officials need to run backwards and sidestep during the course of a match, try to incorporate both of these moves in your training.

Also, Rocky Balboa and Kenyan marathon runners are on to something—running up and down steps or hills helps endurance. In the Rocky movies, Rocky concluded his runs through the streets of Philadelphia with a sprint up the steps of the south entrance of the Philadelphia Museum of Art. Kenyan marathoners run up and down the hills of their country.

Jogging and sprinting up and down some hills or steps will make running on a flat soccer field easier.

Game Day

Take the attitude that you are being given the privilege to officiate your games that day. After all, you will meet new people, have the opportunity to make a positive difference in other people's lives, get exercise and, hopefully, have fun, all while earning a little money.

The game is not about you; it is about the players. Rarely does anybody come to a soccer game to watch the officials; they are there to watch the players. A soccer game could possibly be played without officials but cannot be played without players. Your actions should not make you feel important but should get the players to behave and express themselves fairly.

Refereeing is also not about the money. The best refs bring out the best in everyone, including themselves. With officiating, you can help others while you and they are having fun. If you can earn some money on the side, great!

Arriving at the Field

The referee and assistant referees should come to the field at least 30 minutes before kick-off to have the time to properly inspect the field and teams plus to stretch and warm up. Let's talk about the do's and don'ts of your arrival. **After all, you never get a second chance to make a first impression**.

Officials should be well-groomed with a clean uniform. Arrive at the field with a smile on your face. Perhaps you don't feel like smiling—maybe you don't feel well or did not get a good night's sleep. Smile anyway. It could even put you in a better mood.

Attitudes are contagious. If you're having a very good time, you would be surprised how many other people you are affecting with your positive attitude. That song lyric often comes true, "When you're smiling, the whole world smiles with you."

Never bring your problems to the soccer field as it will greatly affect your refereeing and other people's perception of you.

A major complaint about some referees is that "they are mean." Conversely, I have heard compliments about officials such as "He had a nice smile" or "She had a great demeanor."

Shake the coaches' hands firmly while introducing yourself. Should a coach or player bring up a referee decision from a previous match (which you would not have seen), never criticize a referee or his or her calls.

If a coach is a friend of yours, that coach might converse with you for a couple of minutes. So be sure to spend roughly the same amount of time talking to the opposing coach. Otherwise, that opposing coach could think that you will favor the other team. A referee is the ultimate neutral, and what you do for one team, you do for the other.

Make certain that you wear or take these items to your games:

- Referee shirts. The United States Soccer Federation (USSF) currently utilizes shirts in yellow, black, red, royal blue and Grinchy green. For the new referee, the two most popular colors, yellow and black, should probably be fine as starters. You can add the other colors in both short and long sleeves as you gain experience (and money from your games).

- Referee badge

- Referee shorts

- Referee socks

- Black warm-up suit

- Two whistles

- Yellow and red cards

- Two pens that will not smear if the score sheet gets wet. Or two pencils.

- Score sheet

- Two wristwatches, both with stopwatch and time of day capability. Wear one on each wrist.

- Black referee shoes

- Black shoe polish

- Two assistant referee flags

- Flipping coin. Be certain to use a large coin, such as a quarter.

- Air pump, gauge and needles

- Duct tape to repair any holes in the nets

- Tape measure

- Rule book

- Sunscreen

- Insect repellant

- Band-Aids

- Towel to dry off perspiration and precipitation

- Water cooler

- Fruit

- Cell phone

- Black referee case

You will notice that I have omitted taking a baseball cap to the game. Professional soccer referees certainly do not wear caps during games. Yet they are generally not as exposed to the sun's harmful ultraviolet rays and, therefore, the number one cancer in the United States, skin cancer, as are the many referees who officiate several games on weekends. Wearing a hat is good preventive medicine. Most players and coaches in recreational leagues have absolutely no problem with an official wearing a plain black baseball cap during the game in appropriate weather.

I have worn a black baseball cap for recreational games, the majority of games that I now referee, since the turn of the millennium. But all those years of sun damage built up, especially as I did not wear a cap for my first two decades of officiating, and I developed skin cancer on my scalp in 2013. My one regret from refereeing is that I did not wear a cap sooner.

Wear your uniform to the game. Do not put any item that you wear on the field, such as your watches or your referee shoes, in your case. I have seen many good refs think the equipment was in their case only to find out that it was not after arriving at the field. Finding somebody with a wristwatch with stopwatch capability or with an extra pair of size 10 black referee shoes is difficult to say the least and rather embarrassing!

Level of Games

Many new referees do not realize that it can take years to be able to officiate the most advanced levels of play. As a teenager starting out, I was fortunate that nobody ever pushed me to referee this match or that one. So I was able to develop at my own pace, refining my approach whenever I learned something new.

Generally, assignors have a good idea which level of play that you are able to adequately officiate. If you would like more challenging games or less challenging ones, more matches or fewer matches, speak to your assignor. He or she is there to help you.

You Have the Best View of All the Action

What helps keep me young and enthusiastic about officiating is knowing that even after more than 9,000 games, I routinely see something happen on the field that I have never seen before. Such as:

- Players in the Boys-Under-8 age group chasing a butterfly instead of the ball.

- During a corner kick in a Girls-Under-10 game, an attacking player was making a run to the far post. Just after the ball was kicked, the goalkeeper turned her back to the ball and all the players in front of the goal to watch this other player. The ball landed in front of the goal with the keeper still concentrating on that player.

- A Girls-Under-11 defender kicks the ball near her goal line and loses her shoe in the process. While the opposing team collects the ball, she decides to sit by the goal line on the ground and put on and tie her shoe. The opposing team comes down, crosses the ball and scores with the defender tying her shoe leaving everyone onside.

- A double rainbow over the field after rain in a Boys-Under-14 game.

There are 17 rules, or Laws, in soccer. The only one that can be difficult to comprehend is Law 11: Offside. I'm going to go over each rule in order to help you understand it and its application.

Law 1: The Field of Play

Unlike some other sports, the size of the soccer field can vary.

The field of play must be at least 100 yards and a maximum of 130 yards in length. Fields more than 120 yards are extremely rare. I have never refereed on one.

The minimum width of the field should be 50 yards with a maximum width of 100 yards. I have never refereed on a field more than 80 yards in width.

The length of the field must be more than the width. The field must be a rectangle.

A field that is 100 x 50 yards is legal, so the game will be played. Yet it is extremely small for teenagers or men and women players. The players will be bumping into one another throughout the match. The visiting team may be very unhappy playing on this field. Unfortunately, I've had many games where the field was legal but very small for the age group. You, as part of the officiating crew, must call a tight match throughout the game, plus you must be very alert to avoid getting hit by the ball.

The youngest age groups often use fields that are much smaller. Find out the rules and field dimensions of local leagues before going to the game.

Inspecting the Field

How does a referee inspect the field? He or she walks the field checking to make sure that there are no holes (which would need to be filled in) or puddles (which would need to be swept away). Plus there cannot be any protruding objects on the ground that could be considered dangerous such as sprinkler heads or pitching rubbers. Check also to make sure that there is not any debris such as glass, pipes or rocks on the field. Ask the home team coach to have those dangerous items removed from the field.

Should there be tree branches that hang over the field, discuss with both teams' coaches what your decision would be regarding play if the ball strikes a branch.

Abandoning the match is covered in the rules under Law 5: The Referee, but I will discuss it here with inspecting the field.

I have had situations in which it is raining but the field is definitely playable. Yet twice I had a coach approach trying to convince me that the field was unplayable. Why, when the field that day was clearly playable? It turns out that the team had less than 11 players, the coach was unenthusiastic because of this and was trying to convince me to postpone the match.

While we are on the subject of inclement weather, let's discuss thunder and lightning. It's ironic that Thunder and Lightning are two of the most popular names for youth soccer teams as no soccer game should be played in such conditions. Should you hear thunder or see lightning, you should stop the game—no matter what the score is, no matter how far into the match you are. There are no exceptions, even if people complain about the stoppage of play since the lightning is "miles away."

All officials, players, coaches and spectators are to leave the field area and go somewhere safe such as indoors or inside their cars. You can wait an amount of time to resume play but, per a directive from the USSF, it needs to be at least 30 minutes since the last clang of thunder or bolt of lightning.

Guidelines for safety during lightning in seeking proper shelter:

• No place outside is safe near thunderstorms.

• The best shelter is a large, fully enclosed, substantially constructed building.

• A vehicle with a solid metal roof and metal sides is a reasonable second choice.

If there is no proper shelter, avoid the most dangerous locations:

- Higher elevations
- Wide open areas, including fields
- Tall isolated objects, such as trees, poles or light posts
- Unprotected open buildings, rain shelters, bus stops, metal fences

Regarding visibility of the field such as for approaching darkness, rain or fog, a good rule of thumb to use is that the field is not playable if the referee can no longer see each goal from the kick-off spot.

Do not start a match near dusk if you are unsure if the entire game can be played before dark. Several years ago, after 78 minutes of a Boys-Under-19 game, the game was called because of darkness. The team that was trailing, 3-1, protested since 12 minutes still needed to be played to complete the match; they won the protest and the game was replayed in its entirety. Guess who wound up refereeing the rematch? I did. The teams were at each other's throats before the game as they had very different views as to whether the protest was valid. That was obviously a game that I had to call very tight for its duration in order to keep things under control.

Corner Flags

The corner flags should be not less than 5 feet high with a non-pointed top. Some teams will have flags at the halfway line; these should also be not less than 5 feet high with a non-pointed top. The important item to remember with flags at the halfway line is that they should be placed not less than one yard from the touchline. Many teams mistakenly place halfway line flags on the touchline.

In the past, corner flags were always relatively thick poles. Now many youth teams use flimsy poles and it is difficult to see on which side of the pole that the ball went unless the referee is pretty close to it.

The field should be lined according to this diagram:

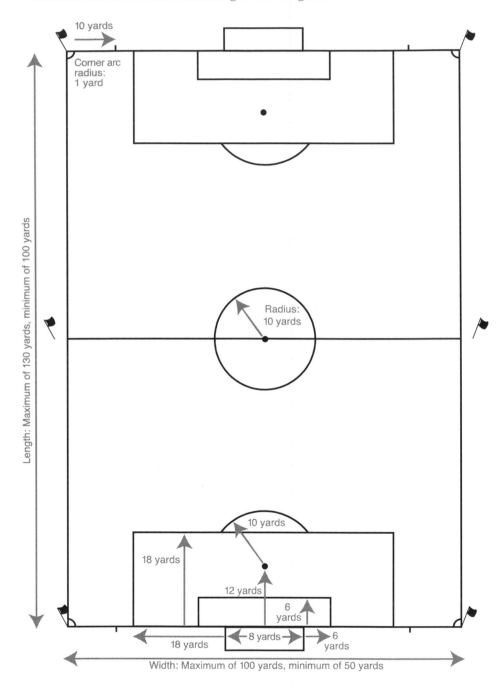

The field of play has 17 straight lines, six other lines that are arcs, one circle and three marks within the field of play plus other markings such as to indicate 10 yards from the corner arc.

Please note that there are 10 yards from the kick-off (the kick-off circle), 10 yards to keep other players from a penalty kick (the penalty arc) and 10 yards to keep opponents from a corner kick (the mark 10 yards from the corner arc). After all, opponents must be at least 10 yards away from every restart in soccer (with the exception of an indirect kick taken less than 10 yards toward the goal that the team is attacking).

The officiating crew should pace off the marks on the field, including those mentioned above, as well as to confirm that the penalty spot is 12 yards from the goal, the penalty areas are 18 x 44 yards, etc. If there's a question as to the legality of the field because it appears quite small, the referee would need to pace off at least 50 yards from the goal line to the halfway line. Keeping a tape measure in your case would be most helpful to determine exact measurements.

If the kick-off circle looks to be 10 yards, pace those yards and count how many of your steps it takes you. Make a mental note, such as 11 of my steps are 10 yards. You will use this info should you need to pace off 10 yards for restarts during the match.

On rare occasions, a referee will arrive at a field that is not lined or where the home team is running out of paint. Which lines are the most important? The vital lines to ensure control for the referee are the straight ones. If absolutely necessary, you can play a game with just the goal line, touchline, penalty areas and halfway line. But be sure to send a report to the league that the home team was not prepared and you should not have the same problem when refereeing at that field again.

The Goals

A very important word about goals, which are 8 yards in length by 8 feet high. The youngest age groups will often use smaller goals. The goal posts must be white. Should you come to a field with goal posts that are not white, play the game and report the color of the goal posts to the league.

Check to make certain that there are no holes in the net that the ball could squeeze through, such as an opening between the net and the crossbar, goalposts or the area between the net and the ground.

Every once in awhile, the official's view of a shot resulting in a goal will not be ideal. Perhaps he or she was screened or was at a bad angle or the sun was in the referee's eyes. Making certain that there are no holes before the game eliminates potential problems on the vitally important task of whether to count a goal during the match.

Interestingly, according to the Laws of the Game, it is not necessary for the goals to have nets. Hopefully, every game that you will be officiating will have them. Only once in my career was I ever confronted with refereeing a match without nets. This is a time when having your cell phone in your referee case with important phone numbers of league officials, referees and assignors is useful so that you can find out what the local league's opinion is of playing a game without nets.

Many portable or temporary goals now have wheels near the front post to help move the goals. When you are checking the goals, make sure that the wheel is pushed back off the goal line.

Most importantly, though, is the fact that the goals must be anchored to the ground. Should the goal not be anchored, the home team or host organization is responsible for placing weights, sand bags, etc. on the back and sides of the goal to make certain that it will not fall over. Should they not do this upon your prompting, **do not start the game**.

To illustrate how dangerous this could be, pick up one goal post off the ground to demonstrate to all concerned how easily the goal can be dislodged. But be sure that there are no players or others nearby when you do this!

A decade ago, I was an assistant referee for a tournament game played near where I live on Long Island. Before the match, I checked the south goal and it was sufficiently anchored. During the first half, the north goal, which had been checked by the other assistant referee (AR), fell over. Obviously, the other AR did not check to see if the goal had been anchored. Thankfully, nobody was hit or killed. The goal was immediately anchored so that the game could continue.

There is no bigger safety issue on a soccer field than falling goals. There were very few fatalities in the 1970s, just a reported two (although that's two too many) in the United States, because of unanchored goals. The number of deaths increased dramatically to nine in the 1980s as more games were being played and more teams were using portable goals instead of permanent goalposts that are anchored into the ground. The 1990s saw 14 deaths and there have been 13 fatalities from 2000 to 2012.

Taking a couple of minutes to check that the goals are anchored upon arriving at the field could save a life and a lifetime of regret.

2

The Ball

Law 2: The Ball

The ball should have a circumference between 27 and 28 inches and weigh between 14 and 16 ounces at the start of the match and can be any color. Check for any tears or cuts on the surface of a ball, which can cut players if sharp enough.

The pressure should equal to 0.6-1.1 atmosphere (600-1100 g/cm2) at sea level (8.5 lbs/sq in 15.6 lbs/sq in). Some pumps come with air gauges. You should have an air gauge to determine that the pressure is correct.

Those are fancy numbers that the players do not know, nor care about. They want to know if the ball feels right and bounces right when it is played.

The information above is for size 5 balls. The youngest players use smaller balls. Size 4 balls have a circumference between 25 and 26 inches and size 3 balls have a circumference between 23 and 24 inches. Check local rules before going to the field.

Decades ago, nobody used to complain about the ball. Today, perhaps since there are different styles of textures, grooves and designs used, on occasion the visiting team will complain. I simply tell them that I checked the ball before the game and it is perfectly fine. When the team realizes that they will have to play with that ball, the complaints eventually end.

Should the ball need to be replaced during the match, such as if it is shot to another ZIP code, the referee or assistant referee needs to check the new ball. If an official did not check any alternate soccer balls before the match, he or she must approve it before restarting play with that ball.

3

The Number of Players

Law 3: The Number of Players

A soccer team utilizes 11 players, one of whom is the goalkeeper. The minimum number required to play is 7 players. The easy way to remember this is to think 7-11.

For the youngest age groups played on smaller fields, teams field less than 11 players. Find out what the league rules are regarding number of players on the field and minimum number required to start the match before going to the field.

Count the Players

The officials are to count the number of players before the kick-off in each half. Do not assume that each team is using 11 players. In rare cases, a team will line up with 10 or 12 players.

I recently saw a Girls-Under-13 match where the officials did not count the players and one team kicked off with 12 players. An assistant referee noticed the discrepancy two minutes into the match. The officials looked very bad after starting a game with 12 players.

Law 3 states that if a team changes their goalkeeper without the referee's permission, play continues and the two players concerned are cautioned when the ball is next out of play.

It will be obvious when the team is changing their goalkeeper during a substitution in either the first or second half. If nobody on the team informs you, ask a player on the team, "Are you switching your goalkeeper?" so that player will inform you by responding "Yes," inferring that permission has been granted.

Generally, teams switch their goalkeeper at halftime. Starting the second half with a new keeper is considered notification.

Also, teams must always play with a goalkeeper wearing a different colored jersey even if that player plays nowhere near the goal.

Law 3 also covers substitutions. In professional soccer, teams are allowed three substitutions, with players leaving the field not allowed to reenter the game. The referee must be informed of the substitution, and the player leaving must be completely off the field before the substitute enters at the halfway line.

In youth soccer, substitutions are unlimited on any stoppage of play. Players being substituted can reenter the game later.

In other regards, the protocol is the same. Substitutes must be standing at the halfway line, dressed and ready to play. The player exiting can leave from any part of the field. To make things easier, the exiting player generally leaves by the halfway line.

In youth soccer, we are dealing with kids—in many cases young children. I have seen referees get themselves in trouble, in insisting that the player leaving the field be absolutely, completely off the field before the sub comes in, by yelling at kids who entered the field a couple of steps too soon.

Let's not make this more complicated than it is. Substitute enters field as the player leaves it. The officials count—one player off, one player on...two players off, two players on.

Do not make the mistake of counting the number of players on the bench instead, which officials have done. For example, the white team has 15 players— 11 players on the field and four players on the bench. During a substitution, instead of counting three players off, three players on, the four players on the bench are counted instead. The officials did not realize that a player just arrived late so the team now has five substitute players, and they are restarting the match with 12 players on the field for white!

Law 4: The Player's Equipment

A soccer player's basic uniform consists of a shirt, shorts, socks, shinguards and footwear. All players should have their shirts tucked into their shorts, including goalkeepers, and shinguards must be completely covered by the socks. A preventive officiating technique is to make sure that the goalies are wearing shirts that contrast with both teams before the match, rather than realizing it at kick-off.

The footwear will generally be cleats, and the referee must check the bottoms to make certain that they are not dangerous, such as having sharp edges. Players may not participate without footwear. However, a goal counts if scored by a player who temporarily lost a cleat.

According to the rules, shinguards must "provide a reasonable degree of protection." Players cannot use shinguards that have been cut in half.

For improper equipment, such as earrings, the referee hopefully spotted any jewelry before the game while checking the teams and no player is wearing it on the field. But if a player wears jewelry on the field, play does not need to be stopped. Instead, the ref waits until the next stoppage in play, then tells the player to leave the field to correct equipment. A substitute can replace the player wearing jewelry. The player with jewelry is allowed to reenter the field when the ball is out of play and the ref has checked that the equipment has been corrected.

Medical alert jewelry or clothing required by a player's religion may be worn only if the referee does not consider it dangerous and it does not give the player an unfair advantage while playing. Medical alert jewelry can often be made safe by wrapping it with tape with the necessary information still showing.

Regarding uniforms, should a player remove his jersey when celebrating a goal, that player is cautioned for unsporting behavior. For the caution to be given, the shirt need not be completely taken off; all that is needed is that the bottom of the shirt to be raised to the bottom of the chin. Players who raise jerseys to display slogans, advertising or messages are cautioned as well.

Regarding arm and/or hand casts, they must be properly covered in sponge and not be dangerous to others for that player to participate.

For complete knee braces, manufacturer's padding comes with each brace and should be worn over it so that there are no sharp edges, which can be dangerous. Some players do not like to wear the padding as they believe it limits their mobility. Have them wear the manufacturer's padding over the brace so they can play.

Some leagues, especially youth ones, prohibit players with casts or knee braces from participating. Ask about this before going to the field.

The Odd Couple's Oscar and Felix

Before we leave the subject of player's equipment, let me state that many leagues have passes for players and coaches which are checked along with equipment and rosters. When checking the player's pass against the roster, mark the players who are there, such as using a checkmark. If the coach says the player will be late, I put an "L" by the name. At halftime, I recheck to see if in fact the player did show up.

Some teams are quite disciplined in lining up: their players are standing in alphabetical or numerical order, the shirts are tucked into their shorts, all socks correctly cover the entire shinguard. The Felix Unger teams.

Then you will check teams that do not seem to care and are an absolute mess. The Oscar Madison teams.

Just as with referees, the attitude of players go a long way in determining the type of match it will be. It will most likely be much more challenging to referee the Oscar Madison teams than the Felix Unger teams.

Instructions to Teams?

When checking the teams, many referees, particularly new ones, make the mistake of telling them how the game will be called.

Saying things such as "When the goalkeeper has the ball, you leave her alone, otherwise I'm going to call a foul" or "Gentlemen, I heard that you don't get along with the other team so I'm going to call a tight match" or any other such instructions is a bad idea and can open a can of worms.

After all, as soon as the ball is legally in play near the keeper and you don't call a foul, the keeper's team will complain that you contradicted yourself. Or as soon as you don't call a perceived foul in a game that you said that you were calling tight, players will complain. Besides, who told you that those teams do not get along?

5

The Referee and Assistant Referees

Law 5: The Referee
Law 6: The Assistant Referee

Let's take these two rules together, in part because the referee and two assistant referees work as a team.

The Referee's Position

The referee's diagonal that he or she runs goes from corner flag to corner flag.

Actually, a referee who strictly adheres to this diagonal will miss seeing a number of fouls. I like to think that the referee's positioning isn't a diagonal as much as it is a **modified** version of a half-open scissor—corner flag to corner flag and penalty arc to penalty arc. The referee is not a slave to this positioning, but it is a rough guide to follow, especially for the newer referee.

I have seen many youth soccer games when the referee made an important call—sometimes correctly, sometimes incorrectly—and loud dissent followed since the ref was 40 yards away from the play. I have seen just as many games in which the call was completely missed by an out-of-position referee. Just as with phones, long-distance calling can be very expensive. The preventive officiating technique is to be fit enough and to hustle each game so that you are close to the play.

Teams are much more likely to dissent from referee decisions when the ref is far away than with the same decision when the ref is 5-10 yards from the ball. After all, presence lends conviction.

Should you blow the whistle for a foul in which you are too far from the infraction, continue running to the point of the restart. You will appear to be closer to the play than the ref who simply blows the whistle and stands there.

During the course of the game, you might encounter 1-2 players on each team who are causing problems. Modify your diagonal so that every time one of these players receives the ball, you are less than 10 yards away. Players rarely commit fouls when the referee is right there.

The Assistant Referee's Position

During normal play for nearly the entire game, the assistant referee's position is parallel with the second-to-last defender. The first defender is almost always the goalkeeper. It is very challenging for new assistant referees to have the discipline to stay with the second-to-last defender instead of watching play develop 40 yards upfield, especially when the ball is in or near the other penalty area. Half the challenge of being an assistant referee is having the discipline to be exactly in the correct position. For example, should the other team take possession of the ball and launch a long pass to your half, you will know if the player running toward the ball is offside by being parallel to that second-to-last defender.

See the diagram on the next page for the position of the officials in the diagonal system of control.

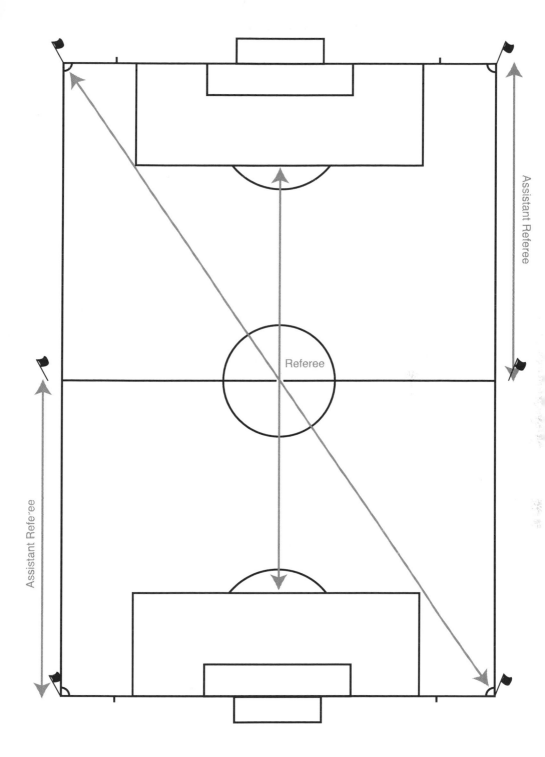

Should 21 players be in the other half of the field with only the goalkeeper in your half, the assistant referee's position is not with the second-to-last defender in this instance but at the halfway line.

Another exception to being parallel with the second-to-last defender is when the ball is closer to your goal line than the second-to-last defender is. Your position would then be parallel to the ball.

Other exceptions are during the taking of a corner kick and penalty kick. The assistant referee's position both times is at the goal line.

On a corner kick, the assistant ref is behind the corner flag.

On a penalty kick, the AR is at the intersection of the 18-yard line and the goal line. But for kicks from the mark (shootouts), the AR is at the intersection of the 6-yard line and the goal line.

Summarizing, the referee's perfect position can vary but the assistant referee's position almost always needs to be exactly in line with the second-to-last defender except with the situations noted above.

How Officials Position Themselves as a Team

Watch professional games and concentrate on the officials, paying special attention to their position and signals.

You will notice that referees like to keep the ball between them and an assistant referee. It's easier to officiate a match when there are two relatively close views, from different angles, of play around the ball.

You'll also see that referees often jog when play is in midfield, such as in or by the kick-off circle, and the ball might be 15 yards away. But referees sprint to get closer to the ball when it is in one of the "hot areas" such as in or by the penalty area or by the benches.

The penalty area is hot since it's by the goal and important goal-scoring opportunities happen there. The area in front of the benches is hot as coaches and substitutes have a close view of play by the touchline and will probably be upset should you miss something against their team.

Running on the Field

Referees and assistant referees need to be in good shape. They spend much of the game running forward.

They might sidestep as well. This technique is fine for the ref to use so that the goalkeeper with the ball is still in view while the ref moves down the field to the area where the ball will land. Sidestepping is also good for the AR to judge offside. However, a "cross-over step," with your legs crossing over each other as you move downfield, can look bad and may make you stumble, so please avoid it.

Running backwards is also important at given times. For the ref, again it's used when the goalkeeper has possession of the ball and is about to distribute it. The referee can also run backwards to prepare for restarts. ARs can run backwards along the touchline when the ball is right in front of them yet they need to move downfield to stay parallel to the second-to-last defender who is in motion. You will notice that players are aware when an official is looking at them and are much less likely to commit a foul because of this. Conversely, I have seen ARs turn their backs to the ball to move down the touchline and a foul was immediately committed.

A reason that a ref should practice moving backwards and to the side when the keeper has possession of the ball is simple: the ref needs to view the ball to make sure the keeper has not dropped it by mistake or the keeper was not fouled, while the ref moves downfield to the area where he or she thinks that the ball will go, sometimes called the drop zone.

All officials should use their ears in addition to their eyes to detect deflections as the ball goes out-of-bounds. ARs can use their ears to concentrate on hearing the thwack of the ball being kicked while looking directly at the second-to-last defender and forwards as well to correctly judge offside.

What Does an Assistant Referee Do?

According to the rulebook, the assistant referees indicate:

• When the whole of the ball has passed out of the field of play

• Which side is entitled to a corner kick, goal kick or throw-in

• When a player may be penalized for being in an offside position

• When a substitution is requested

• When misconduct or any other incident has occurred out of the view of the ref

• When offenses have been committed whenever the assistants are closer
   to the action than the referee (this includes, in particular circumstances, offenses
   committed in the penalty area)

• Whether, at penalty kicks, the goalkeeper has moved forward before the ball
   has been kicked and if the ball has crossed the line

The assistant referee can play a pivotal role in controlling the match, particularly in spotting off-the-ball incidents behind the referee's back. This is why the assistant referee must always concentrate, even when the ball is in the other half of the field.

Let's say that white took a shot that was saved by the gray goalkeeper, who punted the ball to the other half of the field. While running upfield, gray defender #3 punches white forward #10, who falls to the ground. The forward is at the very least stunned, maybe seriously hurt, perhaps this player is now bleeding.

The referee certainly did not see this as he or she was following the play, as was the AR in the other half of the field. Gray defender #3 needs to be sent off for violent conduct and play restarted with a direct kick for striking an opponent where the punch was thrown (and not where the ball was at that time). The trailing AR, who saw the infraction, should raise the flag. If the referee cannot see it, the other AR should raise that flag and after getting the ref's attention, point to the AR who made the important call. If that does not work out, the AR who saw the foul could always yell the ref's name to get noticed.

If the AR misses this serious foul, what type of problems do you think the officiating crew will have for the rest of the match?

When a Referee Overrules the Assistant

The referee can overrule the assistant referee but the assistant can never overrule the ref. The assistant is to *assist* the referee and not *insist* instead.

We have a situation in which the ball has gone over the touchline near the assistant referee, who indicated that it is gray's throw-in. However, the AR did not see the last bounce off a gray leg so it should be white's throw-in instead. The referee should blow the whistle and indicate that it's a white throw by pointing the direction that white is going. The ref should also say something nice to the assistant such as, "Thanks, Bob, but you were screened when the ball last came off gray so it is white's throw." The assistant should then point the flag in white's direction.

A referee should not try to overrule the AR often, otherwise the officiating crew will not be working as a team and the players will realize that the ref has no confidence in his or her assistant—so why should the players?

While overruling the assistant may be necessary on one or two occasions during the match when the ball is out of play, it is absolutely dangerous when the ball is in play.

When an assistant's flag goes up to signal an offside or foul, players tend to stop, even if they have been told to play the referee's whistle, not the assistant's flag. So it is much easier to overrule the assistant while the ball is out of play and do it only when the ball is in play if you are absolutely, positively certain that the AR has it wrong.

Let's take this a step further and mention a Boys-Under-16 game in which I was the AR. Both the other assistant and I were well positioned with the second-to-last defender throughout the match to flag for offside. Yet, the referee decided to whistle for offside when we kept our flag down on five different occasions—two in my half of the field, three in the other AR's half. The game became an absolute disaster! Three players of the losing team were sent off near the end of the game for using abusive language when they cursed the referee.

Before we leave this point, let me just state that referees who want to continuously receive assignments and/or advance through the ranks are going to need to get along with officiating colleagues. Continuously overruling ARs is not the way to win friends and influence people.

Referee's Instructions Before the Match

The teams spend time training and working on teamwork in practice. Their coaches go over tactics before the game. Doesn't it logically follow that the officiating team needs to spend some time before the game discussing how they will work as a team?

The referee should go over what is expected of the assistant referees. I tell them to wait a split second to raise the flag for offside just to be certain that the player in the offside position is involved in the play. A slower flag and correct call is much better than a quick flag and incorrect call.

I also tell them to run all balls down to the goal line.

For good goals, they sprint up the touchline 15 yards or so, watching the players on the field at all times. Should the ball go into the net but the AR spotted a foul or some other problem which the referee did not see (that would nullify the goal), the AR should wait at the corner flag, the referee comes over. They then can briefly discuss what happened and determine whether the goal is valid. This does not include a goal scored by a player in an offside position, as the AR should have already raised the flag and the referee spotted it, whistling for offside.

If the ball goes over the goal line and comes out in one of those bang-bang plays that happen once or twice a year and it's a good goal, the AR raises the flag to get the ref's attention—as soon as the referee sees the flag, the AR sprints 15 yards upfield. This is the only time that the ref blows the whistle for a goal.

The referee should also mention that on out-of-bound plays that occur between the ref and AR, if the ref knows which team's ball it should be, he or she will give a small signal, such as hands on stomach pointing in one direction, so that the AR flags in that direction. After all, the officiating team looks bad when the ref consistently signals the ball one way and the AR has it another way. It's very important for the referee and ARs to have good eye contact with one another.

On throw-ins, the AR can watch for any infraction with the feet up to the halfway line closest to the AR while the ref watches for any infractions with the upper torso. The signal from the AR for an improperly taken throw-in is a twirl of the flag. Past the halfway line, the referee watches for any infraction. You would not want the AR twirling the flag 60 yards away for a foot completely over the touchline in the corner of the field when the referee is so much closer.

ARs should be told to signal fouls within a 25-yard radius of the AR by using the flag as a whistle and twirling the flag. More than 25 yards away, the AR would twirl the flag only if he or she clearly sees an obvious foul that the referee missed.

ARs are also to be told to watch for off-the-ball fouls behind the referee's back.

Should there be opposing players within 10 yards of a free kick near the AR, the assistant should come onto the field to pace off the 10 yards rather than the ref. Play is restarted with the referee's whistle after the opponents are 10 yards from the ball **and** the AR has returned to the proper position.

One AR has the look, the other one has the book. Meaning that one AR watches for the entire game, not putting numbers of cautions or send-offs in the book (score sheet), while the other AR records all this information. At halftime, the officials discuss any numbers in the book to make certain that there are no discrepancies. At that time, the AR with the look records those numbers. The reason that one AR has the look is so that while the ref and other AR are recording the number of a player being cautioned or sent off, retaliation or any other misconduct is not missed.

ARs can also signal if fouls should be cautions (yellow cards) or send-offs (red cards). The signal for a caution is hand over shirt pocket (where the referee keeps the yellow card) and send-off is hand touching back pocket (where the red card is kept). Although there are other AR signals to alert the referee to caution or send off, these are the most accepted ones.

If the referee blows the whistle for a foul near the AR, the assistant should then raise the flag in the direction of the team receiving the free kick. Doing this eliminates the problem of players or coaches saying, "The assistant was right there and did not see a foul but the ref decides to call it from 25 yards away!"

Halftime

Halftime is the interval at which teams, including the officiating team, go over what went right the first half plus what went wrong and how they are going to correct things in the second half. The officiating team as well needs to discuss any potential challenges awaiting them in the second half. An AR could say, "I saw #10 of white and #4 of gray talking to one another after they challenged each other for the ball toward the end of the half. I could not hear them as they were too far away. You (the ref) were running upfield in the other direction at the time. But I don't think that it was a nice conversation. We should watch out for those two fouling one another in the second half and take appropriate action."

A Dramatic Decision

I remember when I made a very important, and correct, entry into an important game as an AR. Two top New York men's teams, Brooklyn Italians and Frosinone, were playing a close match in 1984. Longtime professional referee Gino D'Ippolito was the referee and I was an assistant referee. The score was 1-1 with Brooklyn Italians having a corner kick near the end of the game, in the 89th minute. The ball was headed and landed in front of the goal. During the goal mouth scramble, Brooklyn Italians put the ball in the goal. What Gino did not see as he was screened but what I clearly saw was that during the scramble, as the Frosinone goalkeeper was on the ground stretching to get to the ball, a Brooklyn player tried kicking the ball but missed and kicked the goalie in the stomach instead, helping prevent the goalie from reaching the ball.

I stood at the corner flag, Gino came over and I told him that the goal needed to be disallowed and it should be a Frosinone direct kick for kicking an opponent.

The final score was 1-1.

After the game, a reporter from an Italian-American newspaper, *Il Progresso*, interviewed me. Although I can speak Italian relatively well and have officiated in Italy, I'm glad that we conducted the interview in my native language of English. It took a good deal of courage to make that call.

Player Management

Officials need to approach the game knowing that they will be fair and maintain that attitude throughout the match, no matter what poor or favorable experiences they already have had with the teams that are playing.

It is also very important that the officials listen to the players. Some officials conduct the game as if they are the ultimate power. I have even heard one ref called the "Soup Nazi," from the "Seinfeld" show. Yes, the officials are in control of the game, but they must be approachable to the players.

During the match, the officials must be in constant contact with the players as it makes the game go much smoother. Players and coaches appreciate officials who work hard and care.

I was refereeing a women's match in which there were only five fouls the entire first half. White's center midfielder, #10, was fouled twice during the half and neither were bad fouls, yet she complained each time that she was fouled. I figured that if a problem began in that match, most likely it was going to start with her. So I stayed close to her whenever she had the ball and talked to her and the players marking her a good deal. Presence lends conviction and there were no more complaints from her the rest of the match.

That white team wound up in the semifinal match that I was refereeing. Before the match began, the league commissioner let me know that a player from that team was suspended for being sent off for violent conduct in a previous match. I said to the commissioner, "Let me take an educated guess and say that it was #10." Certainly, I was not surprised upon hearing that she had been fouled and, in her retaliation, got in a very brief fistfight with the player who fouled her.

Attitude Is Altitude

This brings me to the approach of the assistant referees. The ARs, as we have seen, have an important role to play in a game. I have heard many officials say "I'm just the assistant referee for the game." Wrong attitude!

I cannot tell you how many ARs I have worked with who would be much better if they only thought that what they were doing was important and really concentrated. Hard work goes a long way!

In many games, the success of the officiating team's performance often depends upon a critical call by the assistant referee.

The assistant referees are on the side of the field and are obviously closer to the benches and spectators than the referee. Should a coach or substitute complain about a call that the referee made, sometimes it is better to ignore the comment. Other times you can say something such as "The referee was much closer to that foul than either of us" or "The referee had a very different angle than you did."

Never contradict or undermine the referee in any way to coaches, players or spectators. A few years ago, I was officiating a Boys-Under-19 Premier game on a field and heard loud dissent on the adjacent field throughout that Boys-Under-19 Premier match. My game was over first so I watched the last 20 minutes of the other match. The referee was doing a good job. However, I witnessed the assistant referee on the side of the benches making negative comments about the referee to the benches after the ref blew the whistle. This AR committed an ethics violation (see Code of Ethics on pages 107-108). Let's just say that officials who undermine their colleagues are better off spending their free time doing something else!

No matter what the level of the game—whether it's intramurals, travel team, premier, school soccer, amateur or professional soccer—people talk. Officials who work as hard for lower division games as much as they do for Division 1 games plus girls' and women's matches as much as boys' and men's games get good reputations. Officials who take off from a game or two do not.

Since becoming an official more than three decades ago, I have heard complaints about favoritism of certain officials by assignors, referee organizations and leagues. These "favored" officials seem to get many of the so-called top assignments in addition to being assigned games on days when there's little activity. I am certain that organizations and assignors have found these officials to be reliable, to hustle at every game they are assigned and to have forged a good or great reputation. Their hard work is being rewarded.

Whistle While You Work

Soccer referees carry their whistles in their hands, not in their mouths. In raising the whistle to the mouth to blow it, a referee has a moment to analyze a foul to make certain that there is not an advantage situation developing.

To emphasize the use of the whistle when it is necessary to blow it, such as for fouls, offside or close out-of-bounds, refrain from blowing the whistle some other times, such as when the ball was kicked so far off the field everybody can see that it is no longer in play. Or when a team has a kick-off after a goal, simply say, "Play."

If the ball clearly went into the goal, there is no need to blow the whistle; simply point to the kick-off circle. However, the ref always blows it for a goal and points to the kick-off circle on those rare occasions when the ball hits the post, goes over the goal line and then bounces out. You blow the whistle in this bang-bang case so that everyone understands that it's a goal.

A decade ago, I was interviewed by *Newsday* and the article's author, Anne Bratskeir, correctly surmised that "blowing the whistle is an art form." Indeed it is. I often consider my whistle to be conducting a great symphony of players, coaches and assistant referees.

You blow the whistle at normal pitch for common fouls, offside and when the ball just goes over either the touchline or goal line.

You blow the whistle very hard for a bad foul as well as for a penalty kick foul or to disallow a goal. Blowing the whistle hard emphasizes to everybody that you have seen exactly what happened and are going to act decisively.

At the end of each half, you can use one long blow of the whistle or three short blasts in quick succession.

Referees use the pitch of their whistles and their voice for game control plus management of the players and coaches.

How Assistant Referees Use the Flag

Assistant referees are to run up and down the touchline with the flag on the side of the field at all times so that the referee can easily see the flag upon looking at the AR. The arm holding the flag is straight. Always keeping the flag on the field side is not easy because, as soon as the AR changes direction, the flag (which is down by the legs) then must be placed in the other hand. Think change direction, change the hand holding the flag. You might need to practice this technique away from a game situation to get it right. But it will soon become a very good habit that you have perfected.

Just as the referee blows the whistle decisively, ARs raise the flag decisively. Your mechanics should indicate that you are confident in the call.

As we have mentioned, the referee's position tries to keep the ball between the ref and AR at all times. Yet sometimes, this is nearly impossible.

In the United States and in the majority of countries around the world, most refs run a left-wing diagonal, meaning that they will be near the left wing on the forward line when play is in or near the penalty areas. Let's say that the ball is passed by a white player to the white left wing, who starts dribbling the ball near the touchline. Most likely, the ref is not going to be exactly at that touchline and is going to have to see the left wing collect the ball, then turn to see if the AR is signaling offside.

Consequently, the offside flags that are missed are often for situations in which the left wing was offside, as the referee did not remember to turn and look at the AR. In cases such as this, the AR snapping the flag while raising it so that it can be heard by the referee 50 yards away can make all the difference in the world. The bottom line is that if the ref does not spot the AR's flag for offside, the flag continues to be raised until it is noticed. The officiating crew does not look good the longer that play continues.

It is helpful if the referee makes a note of which AR to look at as the ref crosses the halfway line.

Advantage

Advantage is a wonderful clause in the rules in which whistling the foul would actually be hurting the team being fouled by not letting play continue. Let's say the white midfielder is dribbling the ball outside the gray penalty area when a gray player pushes white. Yet white does not fall down and is still able to continue the dribble unimpeded toward goal. The ref yells "Play on!" with both arms extended, indicating to everybody that there's an advantage.

When a team scores from an advantage, I feel as good as the goal scorer for having applied this clause correctly. But just continuing to move the ball upfield is a sign that advantage was applied correctly.

Officials properly playing advantage do a terrific job of letting the game flow, increasing the enjoyment of the game for everyone. Generally, the better the skill level, the more opportunities you will have to play the advantage.

To properly maintain game control, give the proper signal of arms outstretched and yell "Play on!" Also, later try to tell the fouled player, "I saw the hold but did not call it as your team had the advantage" and the player who fouled, "No more holding. I did not call your foul as the other team had the advantage." When you briefly speak to the players later, most of them are very receptive.

When should the officials play the advantage and when should a foul be called? Use these guidelines to help you:

A foul by the attacking team inside the defensive team's penalty area. The ball is so far from the other goal that there is little rationale for playing advantage here. The defensive team would probably much rather have the free kick and get their team in position to receive it upfield.

One item to consider is when an offensive player fouls the goalkeeper who has hand possession of the ball. If the foul was neither a hard nor a deliberate foul and the goalkeeper is still standing, you could play an advantage as the goalkeeper would rather have the option of distributing the ball by punt, drop-kick, throw or dribble than have the goalie's team kick it from the ground by a free kick.

However, you must tell the players involved that you are playing advantage and let the attacking player know that he or she is not to foul the keeper anymore.

A foul by the attacking team just outside the defensive team's penalty area. With nearly all fouls of this nature, do not play advantage. Below is an example demonstrating why.

A gray defender is dribbling outside the penalty area and is tripped by a white forward with the defender falling on the ground. The ball rolls to another gray defender who plays the ball. You yell, "Play on!"

The gray defender then loses the ball to a white forward who passes the ball to a teammate who scores. The gray defender who was fouled and had fallen left that white scorer onside. That is why you rarely play advantage in this situation—the ball is much closer to the goal of the team that was fouled than the other goal.

A foul at midfield. You can certainly play the advantage here, particularly if the team with the ball has open space in front of it.

A foul by the defensive team just outside the defensive team's penalty area. If you see what could be a clear advantage, let them play, as many of these advantage situations with the attacking team going toward the penalty area wind up as goals.

A penalty kick foul by the defensive team inside the defensive team's penalty area. Teams score on penalty kicks most of the time. Only play an advantage here if the attacking player has the ball near the goal with an open goal beckoning.

If the referee plays an advantage for a hard foul, during the next stoppage of play, the player who fouled could be cautioned or sent off. However if this occurs, to help avoid retaliation, yell toward the players involved, "Number three, I saw that foul and I'm going to deal with you when the ball is out of play." Saying the number also helps you remember which player to card a minute or so later.

Should the referee give an advantage but quickly realize that the advantage did not materialize, the ref should blow the whistle and call the original foul.

The Officials Are a Team

Since the officials are a team, they enter and leave the field as one unit—referee in the middle clutching the ball, assistant referees on the side of the ref with the flag to their outside. The more they work as a team, the more they act as a team—before, during and after the game—the more they will enjoy officiating. And the perception of these officials will be much better than an official who wants to be the lone ranger.

Refereeing by Yourself

All this is well and good. But what happens when you referee a game by yourself? After all, many officials referee games without the help of ARs. The great majority of my first 1,000 games were matches in which I was the only official assigned. What do you do then?

A coach once said to me, "Referees seem much more confident when they have assistant referees." Well, of course! Just as the players on his team would be much more confident if they had a full team rather than a depleted squad.

As a solo referee, you should continue to run the field using the half-open scissor that was diagrammed as a very rough guide. But since you are the only official, should many offside decisions need to be made (such as when one or two teams are playing an offside trap), you should stay a bit closer to the touchline than usual, thinking about how the ARs, standing just outside the touchline, signal for offside. The side of the field is the best position for calling offside. Yet if you stay too close to the touchline, you will be in a poor position to call fouls.

Club linesmen, usually the relative or friend of a player, will help you determine when the ball goes over the touchline. Tell them before the game, "Raise the flag only when the entire ball goes over the entire line. Do not give me the direction of the throw as I will determine it."

They are not to signal direction as this can create a perception that they are cheating for the team they want to win. Make sure that you thank them both before and after the game as they are volunteering their time to help you.

No matter if the club linesmen say that they want to help you even more, even if a club linesman says that he or she is an international referee, the only responsibility of the club linesmen is to signal when the ball went over the touchline—not to raise the flag for fouls or for offside or when the ball went over the goal line.

How Do You Look?

On the next few pages are the signals for referees and assistant referees. To get these right, dress in your uniform, stand in front of a mirror in the comfort of your own home and practice these signals and mechanics.

Referee Signals

Free Kick

Indirect Kick

"Play On!" Advantage

Corner Kick

Caution or Send-Off

Penalty Kick

Goal Kick

Assistant Referee Mechanics and Signals

The AR runs downfield with flag always on side of field.

Goal Kick

Corner Kick

Foul, twirl flag

Throw-in

Substitution

Offside. First raise flag above head to signal offside,
then after whistle blows, indicate which side of field...

Offside on far side
of field

Offside in middle
of field

Offside on near side
of field

The Duration of the Match

Law 7: The Duration of the Match

A soccer game consists of two equal halves. A professional match has 45-minute halves while other games could have fewer minutes in the half, depending on the competition or age group. The halves are running time. The time begins when the ball is legally put in play on the kick-off by being kicked forward, not when the referee's whistle sounds.

The rulebook states that time can be added for substitution, injury, time-wasting or any other cause. So if a plague of locusts or some other surreal incident interrupts play, add time.

This is what works for me: I wear two watches, with one functioning as a stopwatch on one wrist and one with time of day featured on the other. Just before the game begins, I look at the time of day on the relevant watch, then write down on my score sheet what the time of day should be when the half is over. So if we are playing 45-minute halves and the game kicks off at 1:02 pm, I write 1:47 in my book. This is my insurance should my stopwatch not run correctly or if I press the wrong button, which occurs on occasion.

When you note the time of day, notice if the minute has almost expired. If so, add another minute in your book so you do not end the half early.

For injuries, I look at my stopwatch when play is stopped, then look at it again when play resumes—always adding the time lost at the end of the half.

In professional games, which have very few substitutions, time is added to the end of each half for each substitution. In youth soccer, there will be many substitutions throughout the match. You do **not** add time for most substitutions in youth soccer.

If the winning team starts substituting a good deal (in order to delay the game), I use a preventive officiating technique and put my fingers over my stopwatch while announcing that the time has been stopped.

If time needs to be added to the half, I announce that as stoppage time is about to begin, "A minimum of two minutes of stoppage time is being added."

The rulebook states that additional time is allowed for a penalty kick to be taken at the end of each half or during the end of each overtime period. To avoid having to disallow a goal after the ball rebounds off the goalkeeper and is then shot in, the referee allows all players to remain on the field, but, with the exception of the keeper and shooter, the other players are moved away from the penalty area. Then the penalty kick is taken.

The referee needs to use some common sense in adding time. If the half is down to a few seconds and one team is attacking in the other team's penalty area, do not end the half until the ball has been cleared, the defense gets the ball or the ball is played out-of-bounds.

Otherwise, you will put yourself in the situation that I found myself when I started as a referee. It was a Boys-Under-12 game with 30-minute halves and, at the conclusion of the first half, as my stopwatch read 30:00 with no additional time necessary, a shot had been taken and was going into the net. Until I unnecessarily became too involved in the game by disallowing the goal as the ball was about to cross the goal line. Do you think that I had a major effort controlling that team's coach during the second half? I sure did!

All of this could have been avoided if I had demonstrated some preventive officiating and a little common sense.

When Players Want to Know How Much Time Is Left

Toward the end of each half, a couple of players might separately ask you, "How much time is left in the half?"

I have actually heard referees say, "I don't have to tell you!" or "Go ask your coach!"

Do yourself a favor. When players or even coaches ask you how much time is left in the half, briefly glance at your watch and tell them. It costs you nothing to answer the question. And you will generally get a "Thank you!" in reply.

Law 8: The Start and Restart of Play

Before the match, a coin is tossed and the visiting team traditionally gets to call heads or tails as a courtesy. As this is the time that you are with the captains, write down their numbers in your score sheet so that if you need to speak with them during the game, you will know who they are, especially if they are not wearing a captain's armband on their sleeve as they are supposed to be doing.

With players 12 years of age and under, I have found that they like to toss the coin. So instead of you tossing it, give your coin to the player on the home team and tell that player to toss it in the air and let it hit the ground. The visiting team calls heads or tails when the coin is in the air. Sometimes, the player who tossed the coin will tell teammates, "Wow, that was cool! The ref let me toss the coin!"

The team that wins the toss chooses which goal they will attack. The other team receives the kick-off.

To begin the second half, the teams change ends and attack the opposing goals. The team that won the coin toss takes the kick-off to start the second half.

At the start of the second half, you might be slightly disoriented after the teams switch sides.

As the referee, as a preventive officiating technique, I will say to myself, "White is now attacking this goal and gray is attacking that goal."

As the AR, I say to myself, "I was signaling when gray was offside in the first half. Now, I'm signaling when white is offside."

The Kick-Off

The kick-off is used to start each half and restart the game after a goal has been scored. After a team scores, the kick-off is taken by the other team.

During the kick-off, the players are in their own half of the field, the opponents of the team taking the kick-off are outside the kick-off circle and the ball is in play when it is kicked and moved forward from the center mark.

After the whistle sounds but before the ball is kicked forward, the opponents cannot enter the kick-off circle nor can either team cross into the other half of the field of play.

If the ball is not kicked forward, the kick is retaken.

If the kicker touches the ball a second time before it has touched another player, an indirect kick is awarded to the opposing team from the place of contact.

Unlikely though it may be, a goal can be scored directly from the kick-off.

The Dropped Ball

A dropped ball restarts the game after a temporary stoppage that became necessary, while the ball was in play, for any reason not mentioned elsewhere in the rules. The number one reason for a dropped ball is after an injury to a player. A dropped ball is also necessary in those rare cases when an outside agent (such as a dog or another ball) causes interference on the field, the ball remains in play after striking the goal post or upright and breaking it or after simultaneous fouls of the same gravity.

A goal cannot be scored directly from a dropped ball.

Whereas professional referees stop the game only for serious injuries, in youth soccer's younger age groups, the referee should stop play immediately for any injury whatsoever. When you call the coach on to the field to attend to an injured player, the coach is there solely to do that, not to coach the team, nor to complain to the referee that poor officiating caused the player to become injured.

The referee drops the ball where it was located when play was halted. The exception to this is when the ball was in the goal area when play was stopped. In this case, the dropped ball takes place on the goal area line (six-yard line) parallel to the goal line at the point nearest to where the ball was located at the stoppage.

Do yourself a favor. Try to avoid stopping play when it's in the goal area, because restarting play can be very messy in front of the goal, as this is an important goal-scoring opportunity off a dropped ball.

A dropped ball must be dropped, not thrown. The referee should hold the ball in the palm of the hand at waist level with the other hand on top of the ball. The ref then pulls away the hand beneath the ball and lets it drop.

Play restarts when the ball touches the ground. The ball is dropped again if it is touched by a player before it hits the ground or if the ball leaves the field after it hits the ground but before a player touches it.

Any player may challenge for a ball, including the goalkeeper, and there is not a minimum nor a maximum number of players required to contest a dropped ball. The referee does not decide who may or may not contest a dropped ball.

Should the goalkeeper have hand possession of the ball when a player is injured, stop play there. Restart play by dropping the ball to the goalkeeper in his or her penalty area after asking the opposing team to do the sporting gesture and not challenge for the ball.

A similar scenario occurs if play is stopped with one team, let's say it is the white squad, clearly in possession of the ball. Before you drop the ball, ask the other team, gray, to kick the ball back to white and drop it at the feet of a gray player.

Teams will generally perform these sporting gestures if you ask them to do so.

The Ball In and Out of Play

Law 9: The Ball In and Out of Play

The ball is out of play when the whole ball goes over the whole goal line or whole touchline, either on the ground or in the air. The ball is also out of play when the game has been stopped by the referee.

The ball is in play at all other times, including when it rebounds from the goal post, crossbar or corner flag and remains in the field of play. Or when the ball rebounds off either the referee or assistant when they are on the field. This is one reason the assistant referee's position is just outside the touchline, so that if the ball strikes the AR, it is out of play.

As a guide, the ball is in play:

Ball in Play	After...
Kick-Off	Being kicked forward
Penalty Kick	Being kicked forward
Throw-In	Being thrown correctly and crossing the plane of the touchline.
Corner Kick	Being kicked
Free Kick	Being kicked
Free Kick (taken inside own penalty area)	Being kicked and goes outside the penalty area
Goal Kick	Being kicked and goes outside the penalty area
Dropped Ball	Touches ground

Another word about the ball being out of play: The referee cannot call a foul when the ball is out of play; however, the ref can caution or send off a player. For example, just before a corner kick is taken, a punch is thrown. The offending player is sent off for violent conduct, but no foul can be called as the ball was out of play.

Law 10: The Method of Scoring

A goal is scored when the whole ball passes over the whole goal line, between the goalposts and under the crossbar, whether on the ground or in the air. The ball does not have to hit the net for a goal to be scored.

Law 10 is the shortest chapter in this book, but let's mention one preventive officiating technique that will help you. Let's say the gray team is winning 3-1 and the white team scores. As soccer uses running time, the white team, which is still losing, might try to get the ball from the net and bring it back to the kick-off circle to save time rather than let the ball stay in the goal.

Should a white player do this, the gray goalkeeper could try to prevent white from getting the ball. Pushing and even a melee could occur. Cautions and possibly send-offs would need to be given.

Avoid trouble by saying as soon as a white player goes for the ball, "That ball is mine. I will bring it back to the kick-off circle." Then take the ball and jog back to the kick-off circle so play can be restarted.

Offside

Law 11: Offside

Now we come to soccer's only confusing rule, offside.

Without the offside rule, forwards could simply stand near the opposing goalkeeper for much of the game, waiting for a pass from a teammate to put the ball in the net. Teams would inevitably drop defenders back to mark the forwards and soccer would cease to be a fluid game of synchronized players moving up and down the field. It would instead resemble lacrosse or Australian rules football.

A player is in an offside position if he or she is closer to the opponent's goal line than both the ball and the second-to-last defender. Please note that the first-to-last defender is almost always the goalkeeper.

Let me emphasize that if the player is level with or behind the ball, that player is not in an offside position no matter if two defenders are not between that player and the goal line.

With this definition of offside, closer to the opponent's goal line refers to any part of the attacking player's head, body or feet being closer to the goal line than both the ball and the second-to-last defender. So if white is attacking, and white's right foot is closer to the goal line than the entire body of the second-to-last defender on the gray team, white is in an offside position.

Please also note that the attacker's arms are not included in considering offside position since an attacking player cannot score with the arms. So if the arm is the only part of white's body that is closer to the goal line than the second-to-last defender on gray, white is in an *onside* position.

A player is not in an offside position if:

- He or she is in own half of field

or

- Level with the second-to-last defender

or

- Level with the last two defenders

There is no offside offense if a player receives the ball directly from a:
• Goal kick

or

• Throw-in

or

• Corner kick

Even though players cannot be offside from a goal kick, offside could possibly be called if a teammate receives the ball directly from the goalkeeper's distribution, such as a punt, drop-kick, throw or pass.

Understand this so far? Okay, now it gets complicated.

It is not an offense in itself to be in an offside position.

That sentence above, which I put in bold, is the source of much discussion and analysis along with the following.

A player in an offside position is penalized only if, at the moment the ball touches or is played by a teammate, that player is involved in active play by:
• **Interfering with play**, which means touching the ball passed or touched by a teammate

or

• **Interfering with an opponent**, which means preventing an opponent from playing or being able to play the ball by clearly obstructing the opponent's line of vision or movements or making a gesture which, in the opinion of the referee, deceives or distracts an opponent

or

• **Gaining an advantage by being in that position**, which means playing a ball that rebounds off a goal post or the crossbar to the player having been in an offside position or playing a ball that rebounds off an opponent after having been in an offside position.

The rules actually state "at the moment the ball touches or is played by a teammate." Offside could be called when the ball is passed or shot or a player receives the ball from a teammate's poor dribble that got away from the player. When a white player is simply and clearly dribbling the ball at his or her own feet, none of white's teammates should be called offside.

Assistant referees are to use the preventive officiating technique of waiting at least a split second before raising the flag for offside to give the assistant the time to correctly determine that the player in the offside position is interfering with play or an opponent or gaining an advantage by being in that position.

For example, let's look at this diagram below.

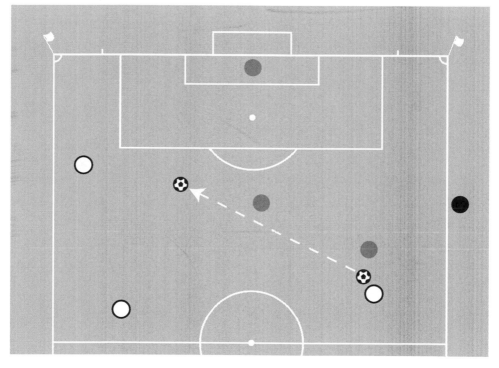

White is attacking. A white midfielder passes the ball toward a teammate by the touchline in a clear offside position. The assistant referee in black is perfectly positioned parallel to the second-to-last defender. The AR correctly waits a split second to review the situation before raising the flag. Now let's move on the next diagram.

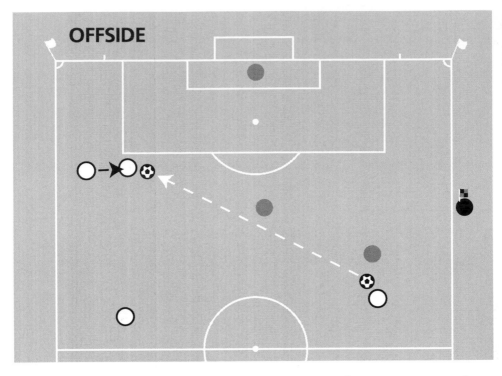

The white forward in the offside position moves to and is going to receive the ball. That's when the AR raises the flag for offside.

Now let's look at what else could have happened on the play.

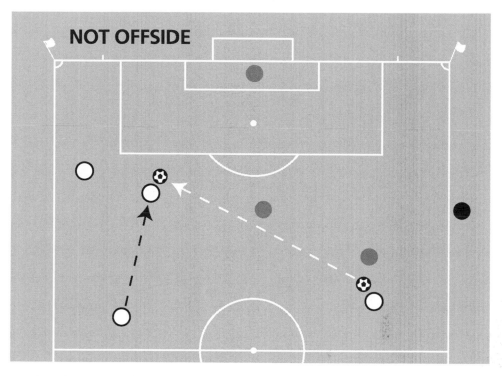

The white forward by the touchline sees that he is an offside position and knows that if he touches the ball, he will be called offside. So he stands still, allowing his teammate, a white midfielder, to run from near the halfway line and receive the ball.

In this scenario, was that white forward standing by the touchline interfering with play or an opponent and gaining an advantage by being in that position? The answer is an unequivocal "no."

So with the AR's flag not raised, the white midfielder receives the ball and is about to dribble into the penalty area for a shot.

The assistant referee allowed this play to happen by waiting that split second to assess the situation and see that the player in the offside position was not moving to the ball but that an onside teammate was. Full credit to the AR!

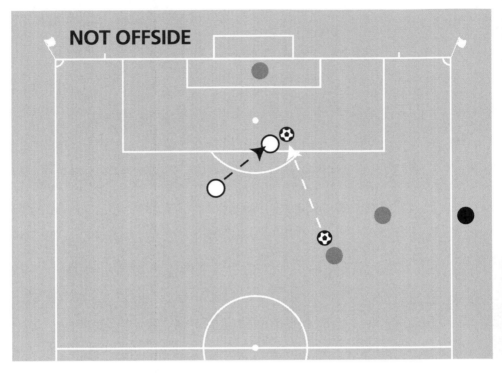

In the above example, a gray defender attempts to pass the ball back to his goalkeeper. The white forward is clearly in an offside position at the time the ball is passed. However, the ball was played by an opponent, not a white teammate, so this play is onside.

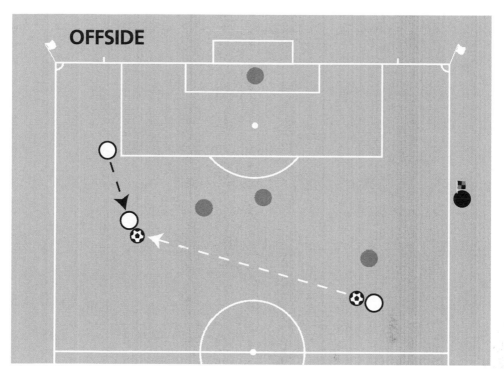

In this diagram, the white forward is clearly in an offside position at the time the ball is passed. Yet he comes back and receives the ball with three opponents between him and the goal line.

However, the rule is when the ball is played by a teammate so white is called offside.

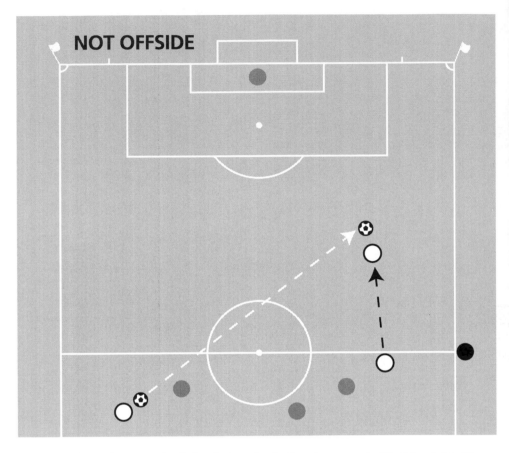

The white player on the left side has the ball in her own half of the field. There is no player other than gray's goalkeeper in the other half of the field.

The assistant referee, correctly positioned right at the halfway line, sees a white forward sprint to the ball from her own half of the field at the time that the ball was kicked. This play is onside and white now has a breakaway.

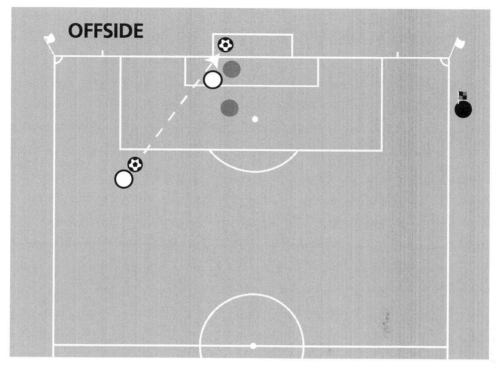

In the above diagram, the white player launches a shot on goal from outside the penalty area. The white forward is standing right by the gray goalkeeper, interfering with the goalie's ability to make a save. Offside is correctly signaled by the AR.

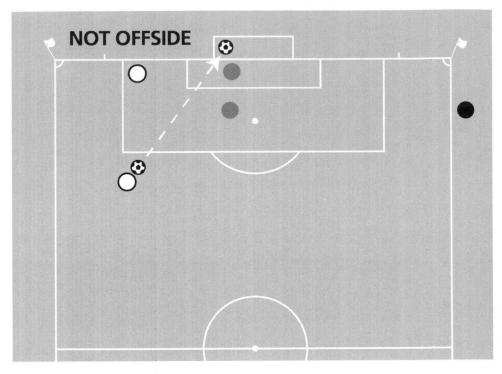

In this diagram, the same player as in the previous scenario takes the shot. The white forward, instead of being by the keeper, is standing 15 yards away but is still in an offside position. In no way is he interfering with play or an opponent or gaining an advantage by being in that position, so offside is not called and this is a valid goal.

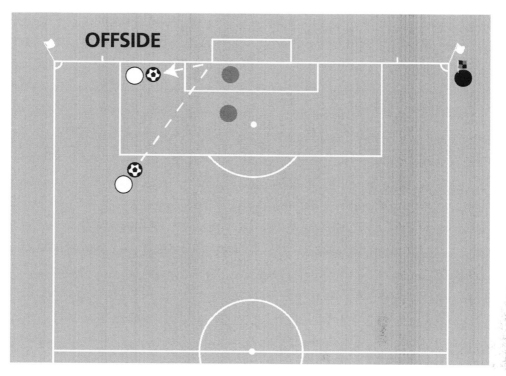

In this case, the shot is taken by the same white player. The other white forward is clearly in an offside position at the moment the shot is taken. But the AR keeps the flag down as white is not interfering with play or an opponent nor gaining an advantage by being in that position.

However, the shot hits off the goal post and rebounds directly to the player in the offside position. Now, the player is offside and the AR correctly raises the flag at this point.

Let's say the players were in the same position, the ball was shot and stopped by the keeper but the ball rebounded to the player in the offside position. Offside would be called in this case as well.

If a defender, in this case the keeper, **deflects** the ball to an opponent who was in an offside position, offside is called. If a defender **passes** the ball to an opponent in an offside position, offside is not called.

To review, it is imperative that ARs have the discipline to be in exactly the correct position, which is nearly always being parallel to the second-to-last defender, and that they have the discipline to wait at least a split second to determine that the player(s) in an offside position should be called for offside before raising the flag.

Before we move from this rule, let me also mention the placement of an indirect kick when offside is called. As soccer's restarts take place where the infraction occurred, the indirect kick takes place where the offside player was standing at the time the ball was played. The only exception is if the offside player was in the goal area (six-yard box); in this case, the indirect kick can be taken anywhere within the goal area.

Law 12: Fouls and Misconduct

Law 12 is the most important rule in soccer. Referees who have played soccer have an initial advantage in spotting fouls over those refs who never played the game. After all, the official who played knows what a foul feels like and might even know what a cautionable or sending off foul feels like as well.

But the referee who never played the game certainly can learn how to recognize fouls as well.

In order to increase fouls and misconduct recognition, officials should watch soccer games, whether on television, video or at a stadium, and "referee" the game along with the officials. I cannot overemphasize how much watching games actually helps officials.

Let me also stress that it is extremely important that the referee call the first foul so that it does not lead to a second. For example, gray #5 pushes white #9 but nothing is called. You can expect gray #5 to be fouled later, most likely by white #9. Call the first foul and you will most likely not have a retaliation foul.

The author blowing the whistle and giving the free kick signal by pointing in the direction of the goal line being attacked.

Direct Kick Fouls

There are 10 offenses, called penal fouls, which are penalized by a direct kick in most of the field and by a penalty kick when committed by the defensive team inside the penalty area. These 10 fouls are:

Kicks or attempts to kick an opponent. But should the player kick the ball first and, in playing the ball, the opponent is kicked as well, this is not a foul as long as the follow-through was not a deliberate attempt to kick the opponent.

Trips or attempts to trip an opponent.

Strikes or attempts to strike an opponent. Striking involves use of any other part of the body except the leg as well as using the ball or any hurled object. Examples are using the elbow or fist. This foul also includes a goalkeeper deliberately throwing the ball at an opponent. If a striking foul occurs, the foul is penalized from where the opponent was standing.

A player who deliberately strikes an opponent is also sent off for violent conduct (if not challenging for the ball) or serious foul play (if challenging for the ball).

Please notice that the three above offenses state "attempts to" do an action in addition to doing that action. An opponent need not be actually kicked, tripped or struck for a foul to be awarded.

Spits at an opponent. As disgusting as this may sound, the saliva does not have to actually hit the opponent for a foul to be called and a red card to be given for spitting at an opponent.

Pushes an opponent. The push can be either a two-hand or one-hand push or caused by using the body, such as the hip.

Jumps at an opponent. Players should at least be looking at the ball to properly play it. Players jumping at opponents, not in playing the ball, are committing a foul.

Charges an opponent. But please note that a properly executed charge is perfectly legal when the ball is within playing distance. The shoulder and the upper arm can be used to tackle an opponent, so long as contact is with the same part of the opponent's body and at least one foot of the player (using the charge) is on the ground. A legal example is shoulder-to-shoulder or upper arm-to-upper arm. Certainly not acceptable is the shoulder into the back or chest of an opposing player, which is a charge and a foul.

Holds an opponent. A player will grab the arm, hand or shirt, sometimes even the shorts of an opponent. Rarely is a part of the lower torso held. This foul also involves a player staying on top of an opponent after both have fallen to the ground. Players do not like to be held and will often retaliate while in the clutches of an opponent if this foul is not called.

Tackles an opponent to gain possession of the ball but makes contact with the opponent before touching the ball. The player cannot make contact with a part of the opponent before touching the ball or go through the ball and then deliberately play the opponent.

Handles the ball deliberately (except the goalkeeper inside the keeper's own penalty area). The challenge here is to determine if the handling was deliberate. A rule of thumb to use is that if the hand or any portion of the entire arm strike the ball, it is deliberate handling and should be called a foul. If the ball instead strikes a hand or arm, it is not deliberate and is not a foul. The exception to this is if a field player has the hand or arm in an unnatural position such as above the shoulder and the ball strikes it, handling should be called.

Goalkeepers who deliberately handle the ball outside the penalty area are whistled for handling as well. The important item to note here is where the ball was, not where the keeper was, when the goalie handled it.

The keeper cannot be standing inside the penalty area and reach outside the area to grab the ball. This is a foul.

However, the keeper can be standing just outside the penalty area and handle a ball inside the penalty area and this is perfectly legal. The 18-yard line is included as part of the penalty area, as the line is part of the area it marks in soccer.

You would be surprised at how many goalkeepers do not know exactly where they can legally handle the ball.

Also regarding handling, instinctive movements of arms and hands of females to protect breasts and males to protect groins is not considered a deliberate handling of the ball.

Indirect Kick Fouls

An indirect kick is awarded to the opposing team if a goalkeeper, inside the keeper's own penalty area, commits any of the following offenses:

While having hand possession of the ball (such as after making a save), the keeper takes more than six seconds before releasing the ball from possession. The keeper needs to punt, drop-kick, kick, dribble or throw the ball to avoid having the infraction whistled. When the keeper has used up almost all the allotted six seconds, the ref should tell him or her to put the ball in play, and most keepers will quickly comply to avoid having this offense called.

Be especially alert of keepers holding on to the ball when their team is winning. After you call a foul in this instance, you can caution the keeper for delaying the restart of play.

The referee does **not** verbally count to six or make any counting movements with an arm when the keeper has possession of the ball.

While having hand possession of the ball (such as after making a save), the keeper releases the ball and then touches it again with the hands before the ball was touched by another player. As an example, the keeper is holding the ball, puts it on the ground and starts dribbling it inside the penalty area, then picks up the ball. This is illegal.

*After pointing for the direction of the free kick, use this **indirect kick signal** and keep your hand raised until the ball is touched a second time.*

A teammate deliberately kicks the ball to the keeper who touches the ball with the hands. This is often erroneously called "the back-pass rule," but the ball does not need to be passed back to the keeper by a teammate. It can be passed to the side and can even be passed forward.

What has to happen for a foul to be called is that a teammate deliberately passes the ball with the foot to the keeper who handles the ball or in the direction of the keeper who moves to handle the ball. Should the keeper receive the ball from a teammate's deliberate pass and the keeper dribbles the ball and then handles it without it touching any other player, it is still an indirect kick.

Should a shot deflect off a defender's foot and rebound to the keeper who picks up the ball, that play is perfectly legal as no deliberate pass was made.

Any other part of the body, such as the thigh, chest or head, is fine for the pass from a teammate.

Please also use a little bit of leniency regarding the deliberate intent of the pass when refereeing young children.

The keeper touches the ball with the hands after receiving it directly from a throw-in.

For your information, the goalkeeper is considered to be in possession of the ball:

- While the ball is between the hands
- While the ball is between the hand and any surface, such as the ground, a goal post or own body
- While holding the ball in an outstretched open hand
- While lodged between the legs after making a save
- While in the act of bouncing it on the ground or tossing it in the air

When a goalkeeper has possession of the ball, the keeper cannot be challenged by an opponent.

An indirect kick is also awarded to the opposing team if a player, in the opinion of the referee, does any of the following:

Plays in a dangerous manner. Often called "dangerous play." Some dangerous play scenarios entail kicking at the ball waist-high or higher with an opponent nearby, showing the bottom of the studs while kicking or tackling the ball near an opponent, heading a ball close to the ground that an opponent is trying to kick plus lodging the ball between the body and the ground with an opponent trying to play it. Please note that an opponent has to be involved near the play for dangerous play to be whistled.

Impedes the progress of an opponent. More commonly called obstruction. Generally, a player cannot use his body to impede another player's movement, even if it is not deliberate. This can be whistled as a foul if a player is not within playing distance of the ball and blocks an opponent's movement or screens an opponent from the ball.

However, if a player is within playing distance and able to play the ball, the player can legally shield an opponent from the ball. This often occurs when a ball is going out of play and the player whose team will get the throw-in, goal kick or corner kick screens the opponent so the opponent can't save the ball.

Prevents the goalkeeper from releasing the ball from the hands. Opponents must not stand in front of or move with the keeper to prevent the ball from being released.

Commits any other offense, not previously mentioned in Law 12, for which play is stopped to caution a player.

When Players See Yellow or Red

Regarding cautioning or sending off players, many things can be in a ref's head when the decision is made to either give simply a verbal warning, go with a yellow card or go with red. Things such as degree of physicality used, behavior of the offender prior to the incident, what the players and coaches are expecting, division level, skill level and where the incident took place on the field. This is all a good deal to digest and will become easier to process as you gain game experience.

Just as with calling fouls, sometimes the decision is clear-cut, but sometimes it is very subjective. On the next page are some guidelines for you to use.

Cautions

A player is cautioned and shown the yellow card if he or she commits any of the following seven offenses:

Shows dissent by word or action. You can let players, especially frustrated players, blow off steam. You cannot let them undermine your authority by constantly complaining about your decisions. Try first to verbally warn them that they need to concentrate on playing, not on the refereeing.

With teenagers and adult players, you could seek a mature captain's help. Hopefully, it's easy to spot a captain as he or she should be wearing the captain's armband on the sleeve of the jersey. You should have written the captain's number on your score sheet before the game to help spot that player. You could say to the team captain, "Your teammate, #6, is constantly complaining about my decisions. I need your help. Either you control him or I will. It would be much better for your team if you control him."

The team generally appreciates the fact that you are trying your best to help their teammate.

If the player continues, you need to show the yellow card. Otherwise others on the field will start complaining since they know it will be tolerated.

Persistently infringes the Laws of the Game. White forward #10 is the best player on that team and the main goal scorer. Seemingly every time that she receives the ball, she is fouled by gray defender #5. Verbally warn that defender that you recognize the pattern and the fouling needs to stop immediately. The captain might be able to help you control her teammate as well. If #5 continues fouling #10, she gets cautioned for persistent infringement.

Cautioning for persistent infringement is also valid if different players take turns fouling white forward #10. If you see this pattern developing, you can verbally warn, then caution the next player who fouls #10. Although technically that caution would be for unsporting behavior.

It's important that all players, especially the teams' top players, are protected by the refs from being constantly fouled so that all are able to play to the best of their abilities.

You can also caution for persistent infringement should the same player commit several fouls against different opponents.

Delays the restart of play. Examples are after a foul is called against his team, a player grabs the ball so the other team cannot quickly restart play, or the keeper of the team in the lead waits a long time before taking a goal kick.

Fails to respect the required distance when play is restarted with a corner kick, free kick or throw-in. A player should be cautioned if he runs up to a stationary ball on a free kick or corner kick, preventing the ball from being put in play. Or he stands exactly at the touchline, where the player trying to take the throw-in is, preventing the ball from being thrown into play, as two yards must be conceded.

Also watch out for players who like to walk by a stationary ball that the opposing team is trying to put back into play on a restart. You can verbally warn first, then caution if the pattern continues.

Enters or reenters the field of play without the referee's permission. As an example, a team decides not to substitute an injured player and plays short with 10. The injured player does not seek the ref's permission to come back on to the field.

Think very carefully about cautioning in this case if the player in question is quite young and just enthusiastic about returning to the game.

Deliberately leaves the field of play without the referee's permission. An example is a defender who runs off the field to try to fool the officials in to calling offside.

Is guilty of unsporting behavior. I saved this cautionable offense for last because it covers so much that offends the spirit of the game. Examples include players taking dives (which rarely occurs in young kids' games), players taunting or mocking opponents, goal scorers raising their shirts to their chin or taking them off completely to celebrate or displaying messages underneath shirts, plus tactical fouls to disrupt play. With a tactical foul, the player who was fouled, often in midfield, cannot continue with a promising attack. This is sometimes called a "good foul" by commentators on soccer telecasts, as it allows the defenders to get back near their goal for the free kick.

Send-Offs

A player, substitute or substituted player is sent off and shown the red card if he or she commits any of the following seven offenses:

Is guilty of serious foul play. When the ball is in play, it is serious foul play if a player uses excessive force or brutality when challenging for the ball on the field against an opponent. For example, a player who lunges at an opponent in challenging for the ball from the front, from the side or from behind using one or both legs with excessive force and endangering the safety of an opponent has committed serious foul play. There can be no serious foul play against a teammate, the referee, an assistant referee, a spectator, etc.

Is guilty of violent conduct. It is violent conduct when a player or substitute is guilty of aggression towards an opponent when they are not contesting for the ball or towards any other person (a teammate, the referee, an assistant referee, a spectator, etc.). The ball can be in or out of play and the aggression can occur either on or off the field of play. An example would be a fistfight starting when the ball is out of play.

Serious foul play and the related offense of violent conduct are strictly forbidden. They violate the spirit of the game and the referee must respond to them by stringently applying the rules.

Referees must be particularly vigilant regarding clear offenses that are too severe for a caution and include one or more of the following additional elements:

- Retaliation
- Tackling from behind
- One or both feet, with cleats showing, above the ground
- Violent or excessive force
- No chance of playing the ball

Violations of the rules which meet these criteria must be called and the appropriate red card must be given.

Please be aware that excessive force, brutality and guilty of aggression are not terms associated with young children. Most likely, the studs-up tackle or tackle from behind was simply an attempt to win the ball.

In 2008, www.BigAppleSoccer.com wrote an article about me in which I said, "What looks like a red card in a pro game might not at the Under-12 level. You have to look at the intent. For example, studs up on a sliding tackle, 99% of 11-year-olds would not know that's a bad foul. A man or woman would. That would be a send-off in those games. At Under-12, you blow the whistle hard and tell them, 'Don't do it.'"

Spits at an opponent or any other person. If a player deliberately spits at an opponent or anybody else, the saliva does not have to actually hit a person for this to be a send-off.

Denies the team an obvious goal-scoring opportunity by deliberately handling the ball (this does not apply to a goalkeeper within his or her own penalty area). This rule applies to the goalkeeper who comes out of the penalty area to deliberately handle the ball or a field player who deliberately handles the ball on a shot that was going into the goal.

Two decades ago, a field player would deliberately handle the ball to prevent a goal and just receive a caution. The number of goal-preventing deliberate handling offenses declined when this was added to the list of send-offs.

Should a young goalkeeper, such as nine or 10 years old, come outside the penalty area and deliberately handle the ball, most likely he does not realize what he did. Whistle the direct kick, think twice before giving a card and the game might be best served by simply telling him to only handle the ball when it is inside the penalty area, without issuing a card.

Please be aware that it is not a send-off, just a direct kick foul, when a keeper makes a save inside the penalty area and his momentum takes the ball outside the area while still holding it.

Should a defender (not the goalkeeper) deliberately handle the ball which winds up going into the goal anyway, you allow the goal and caution that defender for unsporting behavior.

Denies an obvious goal-scoring opportunity to an opponent moving toward the player's goal by committing an offense punishable by a free kick or a penalty kick. This rule is to prevent the defense from fouling to destroy their opponents' most dangerous scoring opportunities. Per a 2002 USSF position paper, there are four required elements for an obvious goal-scoring opportunity before the foul becomes a red card offense and these are described as the four D's:

- **Defenders:** Not counting the player committing the foul, there is at most one opponent between the foul and the goal. That other opponent is generally the goalkeeper. The keeper can be sent off for this offense as well.

- **Distance to the ball:** The attacker must be close enough to the ball to continue playing it at the time of the foul.

- **Distance to the goal:** The attacker must be close enough to the goal to have a legitimate chance to score. So being in or near the opponent's penalty area is more likely to be an obvious goal-scoring opportunity than the attacker being in the team's defensive half of the field.

- **Direction:** The attacker must be moving toward the opponent's goal at the time of the foul, not toward a corner flag or away from the goal.

Uses offensive, insulting or abusive language and/or gestures.
Unfortunately, I am sending off players for this reason more than ever as kids and young adults today grow up commonly using curses in ways that older generations never even considered. If a player obviously curses at a person during the game, the player is sent off.

If a player uses a slur, such as a racial or religious slur, the player is sent off.

Receives a second caution in the same match. Two cautions in the same game equal a send-off. The referee displays a yellow card, then a red card.

Do not get in the bad habit of not giving a player a second caution if it is warranted. Too many referees allow a player already cautioned to commit what would be another cautionable offense without showing the second yellow card, then displaying the red card. They simply call the foul and leave the player in the game, hurting their game control.

"Could You Give Us the Player's Pass Back?"

In leagues with player passes, you might be approached by the coach or team captain after the game to ask that you give the pass back to the team. I have heard such comments as "He really did not mean to do that" or "Don't you think that you could have given a yellow card instead?" The team does not want you to take the pass, write a report about the incident and have their player suspended.

Don't give the pass back to the team. To illustrate why, I will mention an infamous incident from the 1980s at the historic Metropolitan Oval in New York City as a referee was physically assaulted by three players on a men's team. It turns out that one of the players involved was sent off the week before and the referee gave his pass back to the team and never reported the incident. That referee wound up in a great deal of hot water.

That is an extreme example, but giving passes back allows players who should be suspended back on the field to make the game difficult for the next referee. Players need to learn that they are responsible for their actions and will be punished accordingly.

How Many Players Are Left?

One of the great things about soccer's rules is that players who are sent off are not replaced. Their team must play short-handed (really "short-footed") for the rest of the match. So if a player was sent off after the kick-off, including during the halftime interval, the team plays one player short.

Should a player somehow manage to get sent off before the game (and wouldn't that be an interesting game report to wind up writing!), the player may be replaced by a substitute.

Teams do not have to lose a player on the field when substitutes who are not playing in the game are dismissed. I've been lucky; that has never happened in any of my games.

How to Caution and Send Off Players

I wrote about the why's, now let's discuss how to display cards. It is not a good mechanic when the referee displays the card to a group of players. Which player received the caution? Who was sent off? Inquiring minds want to and need to know!

Should there be a group of players standing together, the referee isolates the player in trouble, so that there is no confusion as to who is receiving the card.

The referee walks up to the player, perhaps has a word for a few seconds as to the reason for the caution or send-off, then displays the card high over the referee's head.

Do not demand that the player to be carded approaches you as this is abusing your authority and makes you seem dictatorial.

When cautioning and sending off—as well as any time you are on the soccer field—do not point a finger at the player and never, ever lose your cool. A referee must be cool, calm and collected at all times. If everybody else is losing their cool during a tempestuous match, don't fall into the trap of doing the same. The officials certainly cannot control the game if they lose control of themselves.

Coaches

In the early 1990s, the college referee chapter in which I was for many years a Vice President, NYMISOA (New York Metro Intercollegiate Soccer Officials Association), started a sportsmanship award.

Each official was sent a ballot. The instructions said to grade the coach of that team of squads we officiated during the season on the scale of one to 10—one for none or a very small amount of sportsmanship and 10 for much sportsmanship.

I read the instructions incorrectly and started grading the players of the teams instead. After nearly completing the form, I realized my mistake so I crossed out my answers. In now grading the coaches, my points mimicked what I had written for the players of those teams. In nearly all cases, the points were exactly the same! So if I had given a seven for the players of State U., the coach received a seven as well.

The lesson to be learned here is how much coaches influence the conduct of their players. And these were college players, most of whom had been playing soccer for a decade or more. Youth players with less experience playing plus in life in general should be even more impressionable.

Think of how much time a coach spends with players. Certainly, the coach's attitude toward referees and others can rub off on the players.

Also, regarding dissent, a player unhappy with the ref's decision is sometimes standing nearby and generally does not have to yell to be heard by the referee. A coach, however, is by the touchline and the ref is often in the middle of the field. The AR on the bench side can be far away as well. In order to be heard by the officials, the coach generally has to yell. Nearly all the players on the field and all the substitutes on the benches plus the opposing coach will hear why the coach is unhappy. Allowing the coaches to give a running commentary on the officiating hurts the discipline of the match.

Therefore, **the conduct of coaches is an extremely important factor in controlling the game.**

Thankfully, most coaches are very well behaved. They are there solely for their players and to teach them skills plus give them positive life experiences.

Yet there are those coaches who treat every game as if it was the World Cup final. Their coaching career generally follows this pattern: Son or daughter wants to play organized soccer and parent decides to coach this new team, which could be Under-6, Under-7, etc.

Coach may have experience playing soccer, maybe not. Coach is very intense, particularly during games. He or she will yell throughout the match, not comprehending that these are young children wanting to have a good time playing soccer, not Marine recruits that the coach has to whip into shape. You could say that he or she is living life vicariously through his kids. With all this yelling and the coach's attitude, you get the impression that the coach believes only he or she knows anything about soccer.

After the coach starts yelling at the team's players, the coach eventually gets around to screaming at the referees. This coach does not respect the referee's authority and also does not respect others.

I started refereeing when I was 16 years old and encountered this type of coach on occasion. I still do! These coaches who are much too intense for their players and just about everybody else are almost always in the youngest age groups. If they make it up to their players becoming Under-16, the coach generally has learned and the attitude most likely has dramatically changed for the better. After all, kids who are constantly yelled at lose their enthusiasm for the game, quit in a few years and often the team folds.

Yet, as mentioned, the great majority of coaches are well behaved and are there solely for the players. They are at the very least relatively comfortable with where they are in life. They will start coaching a son or daughter as a young child and continue as the players become teenagers.

When that team graduates from high school, the coach is still enthralled with the soccer bug and the positive effect he or she had on players. Coach will often move on to coaching another young team, whether any of the players are related to the coach or not. By this time, that coach has established a positive reputation and might even be paid by parents for coaching and training their children.

The coach moves on to coaching other teams too and maybe grandkids one day.

This Survival of the Fittest continues as the bad coaches are weeded out or quit and the good ones often coach multiple teams across generations. This is what has happened on Long Island and is one reason why the island is and remains a soccer hotbed and is known for developing excellent players.

I never encountered a problem coach many years later at a game but my schedule each season is chock full of teams with good ones who have coached numerous squads through the years.

Keeping Control of Coaches

So how do the officials control coaches who need to be controlled?

Soccer's world governing body, FIFA (Fédération Internationale de Football Association), says that the coach is not to be shown a yellow or red card, unlike the players. A coach can simply be dismissed.

What I would do in this case is if the coach starts yelling at or constantly complaining to any of the officials, **ask** the coach to modify his or her behavior. If it continues, nicely and calmly **tell** the coach, "Coach, let us concentrate on officiating the game and you concentrate on coaching your players. Otherwise, I'm going to have to tell you to leave."

Should the coach continue, **dismiss** the coach. No exceptions! If you do not dismiss the coach, you will most likely lose control of the match, in part because you did not do what you said would happen. Plus that coach will think that he or she can yell at officials with impunity and will probably do the same to the officials at the team's next match. In fact, you could be receiving the effects of a coach who is a yeller and possibly a referee-baiter but who has gone unpunished up to this point.

Upon dismissal, the coach must leave the field area for the duration of the match. The locker room or a distant parking lot would be a good place for the coach to go.

Should the coach refuse to leave the field area, simply tell him or her, "Coach, if you refuse to leave the field area, I will be forced to terminate this match because of your actions."

Then terminate the match if the coach still refuses to leave.

Write a report about why the coach was dismissed and send to the appropriate authority for their review, including any inappropriate comments or actions by the coach after dismissal.

Most leagues have passes. With these leagues, it's likely that a coach is sanctioned by a referee displaying yellow and red cards, just like the players. Check with the league or your referee association first before officiating the game.

In these leagues, follow this protocol: Verbally warn a coach in a nice and calm voice after he or she starts yelling at an official or constantly complaining about the calls. Some coaches will stop at this point.

If the coach continues, display the yellow card for dissent. The great majority of coaches will stop after that.

Yet a few coaches are not going to keep control of themselves. Should any coach continue yelling, display the yellow card, then the red card for receiving a second caution in the same match.

Should a coach curse at an official, the other coach, an opposing player or one of his own players or a spectator, the coach is immediately dismissed for using offensive, insulting or abusive language and/or gestures.

Again, most coaches will be very well behaved. A small percentage of coaches will not be and they need to be controlled. Control them, control the game. Don't control them, the match will most likely become out of control.

Follow and enforce the rules, and you will be surprised how much support you receive. The league, after reading your game report, will suspend the coach.

You might also receive support from people at the field. After all, people do not like it when others curse or constantly complain, especially if it's in front of their own children.

Let me give an example from a recent Boys-Under-11 game that I refereed. The coach started yelling at me at the opening kick-off. Certainly, I could not allow that to happen throughout the match and retain control of the game. The coach yelled at me again so I asked him to please concentrate on coaching his team rather than concentrating on the officiating.

The next time he yelled, which was near the end of the first half, I cautioned him for dissent. (This was a league in which the coach has a pass.)

What do you think happened then? Nothing, absolutely nothing! The coach might not have been too happy about it, but he kept quiet the rest of the match. He knew that if he continued to dissent, he would have been sent off for receiving his second caution in the same match.

Several months later, I refereed a different team from the same club but with that same coach. He did not dissent at all and just coached his team. He knew that I would not tolerate dissent from him. The game was easy to referee.

Captains

As I have written, captains who are mature can play a very important role in controlling the conduct of teammates. Although the captain has a degree of responsibility for the behavior of his or her team, the captain has no special status or privileges under the Laws of the Game.

I was refereeing a men's game and the captain was unhappy with one of my decisions. He cursed at me. So he was sent off in just the 16th minute for using abusive language.

He then said to me, "I'm allowed to say whatever I want to you as I'm the captain."

It's hard to fathom that he actually believed that. And no, that captain was not mature!

Spectators

Many spectators have no idea what the rules say, especially in youth soccer, and the only soccer matches that they have ever seen are their son's or daughter's. The great majority of problems with parents are avoided by officials who hustle, smile, are approachable, get calls correct plus briefly explain decisions that need to be explained.

Over the course of your officiating career, you will come across that rare human being who has very little experience with the game yet thinks he or she is an authority on the rules and does not respect your calls or whatever brief explanation you may give. Just smile and move on.

But what if that spectator continues to yell? Once you figure out which team the spectator is rooting for, you could seek that coach's help to control the spectator. Some youth leagues require that the coach control poorly behaved spectators. If the spectator(s) continue the poor conduct, the coach receives a yellow card and later a red card if the poor conduct continues. Explain to the coach that the game will need to be terminated if the conduct persists. Should the conduct persist, the referee terminates the match and files a report.

The referee should not confront the spectator as this will only add fuel to the fire.

Thankfully, spectator behavior rarely gets to that level. I can only recall abandoning one of my games because of poor spectator behavior.

Different Age Groups

With the youngest age groups, such as Boys-Under-7, Girls-Under-9 and Boys-Under-11, the potential challenges to game control are generally not the players who are mainly concerned with running up and down the field, kicking the ball and being with their friends, but with the adults—coaches and spectators.

Sometimes, very few spectators show up for games of older teenagers, men and women. The coach must be kept under control, if need be, but the challenge to game control in these matches often is the players.

Consistency and What to Watch Out For

To establish game control during the first 15 minutes of a game, the referee should whistle relatively minor offenses so that the slight push does not become a bigger push a few minutes later.

Officials acting decisively and correctly for an important call, such as a penalty kick, disallowed goal or caution, have done a terrific job and made the game much easier to officiate than if this important call was missed. Referees often talk about the moment of truth in the match when the control of the game was hanging in the balance. The truth regarding this "moment of truth" is that some games have them and some do not.

Particularly in tough games, be a rhino—take charge, be unafraid and have a thick skin.

Red card offenses are send-offs, whether they occur in the third minute or the 90th minute. The 10 penal fouls, when committed by the defense inside the penalty area, are penalty kicks whether they occur at the beginning of the game or the end. Referees who lack courage and give cautions for what should be send-offs and move the ball outside the penalty area for fouls that occur just inside it will have a tough time for the rest of the match. Do not be surprised if the players, realizing that no penalty kicks are going to be called that day, turn the penalty area into a war zone.

Think of attending a speech. The decisive speaker who speaks looking directly at the audience in enthusiastic tones can command the room. The speaker who looks down and stumbles over words or speaks in a monotone or a whisper will make the audience bored very quickly. Which type of speaker would you like to be? And which type of referee would you like to be?

Goals

Play becomes more physical and fouls often occur after goals. The team that scored is energized and perhaps the team that gave up the goal is frustrated. Especially be on your toes after a goal.

Player Fatigue

It takes stamina to play (and referee!) a sport like soccer, which is a wonderful cardiovascular exercise. You will soon recognize signs of players growing tired—players huffing and puffing on the field or asking you how many minutes are left in the half when there is a great deal of time left.

As players fatigue, the game tends to become easier to officiate as there can often be fewer challenges on the ball and the fouls that are committed tend to be obvious. All because of tired players.

Numbers Behind Fouls and Cards

Many professional games have an average of 25-30 fouls during the 90 minutes of play. That's one foul every 3-4 minutes. That's a good barometer to use on how many fouls could be called.

If you called 50 fouls during 90 minutes but issued no cards, probably a caution or two at the very least would have calmed things down. And less fouls could have been whistled the rest of the match.

Should you caution 10 players without a send-off during the course of the match, the players will eventually realize that you do not have the courage to send off a player. Not good for that match and not good if you referee that team a few weeks later. Having said that, there is no magic number of cautions before it is necessary for the ref to use the red card to control the game.

And if the referee distributes cards without any reasoning behind them, then that could add fuel to the fire. I have seen referees lose control of rather easy games as they gave many cards for rather bland fouls and got the players and coaches angry.

13

Free Kicks

Law 13: Free Kicks

Free kicks received their name as they are free from interference by opponents. They are either direct or indirect. For both kinds of kicks, the ball must be stationary when the kick is taken. The ball is in play once it has been kicked and moves.

The Direct Kick

If a direct kick is kicked directly into the opponents' goal, a goal is awarded.

If a direct kick is kicked directly into the team's own goal, a corner kick is awarded to the opposing team.

The Indirect Kick

If an indirect kick is kicked directly into the opponents' goal, the goal is disallowed and a goal kick for the opponents is awarded. The ball must touch another player, either on the attacking or defensive team, before it enters the goal on an indirect kick.

If an indirect kick is kicked directly into the team's own goal, a corner kick is awarded to the opposing team.

An Important Signal

The referee indicates an indirect kick by raising an arm above the head. The ref keeps the arm there until the ball has been touched by another player or the ball goes out of play.

Many players do not know which infractions are penalized by a direct kick and which ones result in an indirect kick. So they will ask you before the kick, "Is this a direct kick?" or "Is it an indirect kick?" Simply tell them.

Where Is the Free Kick Taken?

Except for fouls in the goal area, the proper restart position for a free kick is where the foul was committed. It does not have to be exactly on that same blade of grass (or turf).

The further you are from the goal that would be attacked, the more leeway you could give the team when placing the ball. So if you called offside near the penalty area and the indirect kick is 80 yards from the goal that would be attacked, you can give a couple of yards of leeway to place the ball. Give less leeway for free kicks 20 yards from goal.

Free Kick Outside the Penalty Area

The ball is in play when it is kicked. All opponents are at least 10 yards from the ball until it is put in play.

Free Kick Inside Penalty Area

For a free kick to the **defending team**, all opponents must be outside the penalty area and the ball is in play only when it goes beyond the penalty area, just as in a goal kick. Additionally, all opponents must be at least 10 yards from the kick.

A free kick awarded in the goal area is taken from any point inside that area.

For a free kick to the **attacking team**, the only free kick that could be taken inside the penalty area is an indirect kick. After all, a penal (direct kick) foul inside the penalty area is a penalty kick.

Should the ball be 10 yards or more from the goal, all opponents remain at least 10 yards from the ball until it is kicked.

Should the ball be less than 10 yards from the goal, the opposing team can line up less than 10 yards away if they are standing on the goal line between the goal posts.

For an indirect kick awarded to the attacking team inside the goal area, the kick is taken from the six-yard line at the point nearest to where the infringement occurred.

Referee Mechanics on Free Kicks

Generally, restarting play will not be challenging on free kicks when the ball is far from the goal. However, you will find certain forwards and midfielders deliberately walk by the ball after a foul is called against their team. They are trying to delay the other team restarting play. Do not let them do this—verbally warn them that if they persist, they will be cautioned.

Should a player deliberately run up to a stationary ball, preventing a free kick from being taken, that player should be cautioned immediately for failing to respect the required distance when play is restarted with a free kick.

More challenging is restarting play when a free kick is in or near the defensive team's penalty area. Opponents stand near the ball and prepare to set up a wall. You need to have the defenders quickly move from the ball. If the offensive player(s) ask if they want 10 yards, the referee points to the whistle and yells so everyone can hear, "Wait for my whistle."

You as the referee then back up 10 paces (yards), always watching the ball to make certain that it is not moved. You then call the defensive wall to where you are.

Take your position as soon as possible, glance at the AR to make sure he or she is in the proper position and is not trying to communicate with you, then blow the whistle for the kick to be taken.

Players in the wall can jump up and down but cannot wildly gesticulate. A player doing the latter should be cautioned for unsporting behavior.

It's always a bit of fun when the attacking team decides to put a player or two in the wall. Defenders do not like them there and pushing often occurs. Attackers sometimes try to back up into and/or push defenders to move the wall back further. Watch out for these actions.

Remember that if the ball was not kicked yet when a push, or worse a punch, occurs, you cannot call a foul but you should caution for unsporting behavior (deliberate push) or send off for violent conduct (punch). Should this occur after the kick is taken and the ball is in play, feel free to call a foul plus a caution or send-off too.

14

The Penalty Kick

Law 14: The Penalty Kick

A penalty kick is awarded against a team that commits one of the 10 penal fouls inside its own penalty area and while the ball is in play.

The referee takes the ball, goes to the goal line, and especially if these are young kids who might not know this rule, says to the goalkeeper, "You can move back and forth on the goal line but your feet must be on the line until the ball is kicked."

The referee need not pace off the 12 yards to the penalty mark as this should have been checked before the game. The ref walks to the penalty mark and hands the ball to the kicker, allowing the shooter to position it on the penalty mark. This also serves the purpose of properly identifying the kicker to the goalkeeper.

The goalkeeper remains on the goal line, facing the kicker and standing between the goalposts until the ball has been kicked. As mentioned, the keeper is allowed to move back and forth on the goal line before the kick is taken.

All players other than the kicker and keeper are outside the penalty area, outside the penalty arc and behind the penalty mark.

Along with the start of play from the kick-off at the beginning of each half, the penalty kick is the other restart in which a referee's whistle is required. Before blowing the whistle, a preventive officiating technique that the ref could use is to ask the keeper if he or she is ready and then check again to make sure all players are properly positioned.

The kicker, in approaching the ball, is allowed to stutter-step or hesitate. The kicker cannot fake to kick the ball, completely stop, then kick the ball in the other direction. Or run over the ball, then step back to kick it. If either of these scenarios occur and the ball is kicked into the goal, the kick is retaken and the kicker is cautioned for unsporting behavior.

Let's go over the possible scenarios that occur with a penalty kick:

No infractions by defensive or attacking teams, kick is taken and:

Ball goes into goal. A goal is scored.

Ball misses goal and goes over goal line. Goal kick.

Goalkeeper makes save, parrying the ball over the goal line. Corner kick.

Goalkeeper makes save, does not hold on to ball, kicker or any other player scores on rebound. A goal is scored.

Ball hits crossbar or goal post, rebounds to kicker who puts ball into goal. No goal, indirect kick to defensive team as ball was played twice on restart before touching another player.

Ball hits crossbar or goal post, rebounds to player other than the kicker who puts ball into goal. A goal is scored.

Got that? Now let's go over some other scenarios.

An infraction by the defensive team, such as defender moves into penalty area or goalkeeper moves off the goal line before the kick is taken:

Ball goes into goal. A goal is scored.

Shot misses goal completely or goalkeeper makes save. Penalty kick is retaken.

An attacking player comes into the penalty area before the kick is taken:

Ball goes into goal. No goal, penalty kick is retaken.

Shot misses goal completely. Referee stops play and restarts match with an indirect kick from the place where the infringement occurred (where player was in penalty area when kick was taken).

Goalkeeper makes save. Referee stops play and restarts match with an indirect kick from the place where the infringement occurred (where player was in penalty area when kick was taken).

Ball rebounds from goalkeeper, crossbar or goal post and is touched by this player. Referee stops play and restarts match with an indirect kick to defensive team.

An infraction by both teams before the kick is taken:

Kick is retaken no matter whether the ball goes into goal or not.

Finally, let's use some common sense regarding any of these infractions. Should you believe that a goalkeeper might have moved a silly millimeter off the goal line or players brushed the 18-yard line before the kick was taken, keep the whistle out of your mouth.

15

The Throw-In

Law 15: The Throw-In

The throw-in is unique as it's the only opportunity for players other than the goalkeeper to legally use their hands. It is also the most common restart in soccer.

A goal cannot be scored directly on a throw-in.

A player cannot be offside on a throw-in.

A throw-in is awarded when the whole of the ball passes over the touchline, either on the ground or in the air. The opposing team of the player who last touched the ball receives the throw-in from that point on the touchline. Any player on that team can take the throw-in, including the goalkeeper.

Often, players will not have a very good idea where the ball went over the touchline and some are trying to cheat by moving up the touchline. Not taking the throw-in from the correct place on the touchline is an illegal throw and the throw-in would be awarded to the other team.

A preventive officiating technique is for the referee to stand parallel to where the throw-in should be taken and tell the thrower, "The throw-in should be in line with me."

At the moment of delivering the ball, the thrower faces the field of play, has part of each foot on the touchline or on the ground outside the touchline, uses both hands plus delivers the ball from behind and over the head. It is possible for the majority of one foot or both feet to be clearly on the field of play as long as some small portion of both feet are still touching the line.

Some people are under the mistaken impression that a properly thrown ball will not spin. This is not correct. A player can throw the ball with both hands over the head and it does spin; as long as the motion is from behind and over the head (and not the side of the head), this is fine.

The ball is legally in play if the ball is thrown correctly and crosses the plane of the touchline. Should the ball not do this, the same team throws in the ball again from the same spot.

Let's say that the thrower lifted the back foot while throwing the ball, but the ball never entered the field of play. The officials cannot call an illegal throw-in as the ball was not in play. Retake the throw-in.

The thrower may not touch the ball again until it has touched another player. The restart should this occur is an indirect kick to the opposing team from that spot.

To not impede the thrower, all opponents must stand no less than two yards from the point where the throw-in is taken. Where necessary, the referee or assistant referee should tell any opponent to back off beyond this two-yard distance before the throw-in is taken. The ref would caution the player for failing to respect the required distance on a throw-in, if the player fails to retreat. Play would then be restarted with a throw-in.

Finally, regarding throw-ins or any other out-of-bounds plays such as corner kicks and goal kicks, sometimes the officials have no idea whose ball it should be. If you are completely unsure, wait a second for the player whose restart it should be to go after the ball while the opponent backs off. Thankfully, most players are honest, especially in youth soccer.

If you receive no reaction from the players as to which team should get the restart, maybe they do not know themselves. Pick a team, make your signal decisive and you should not have a problem.

Law 16: The Goal Kick

A goal kick is awarded when the whole ball, having last touched a player of the attacking team, goes over the entire goal line, either on the ground or in the air, and a goal was not scored.

The stationary ball can be kicked from anywhere inside the goal area, which extends six yards from the goal, by anybody on the team including the goalkeeper.

All players of the opposing team must be outside the penalty area. The teammates of the kicker can be anywhere on the field.

A goal can be scored directly from a goal kick only against the opposing team, meaning that it would go into the goal in the other half of the field.

The ball is in play when it has gone outside the penalty area either on the ground or in the air. If after the kick is taken, the ball is touched before it clears the penalty area, the goal kick is retaken.

A reminder that should the ball go directly from a goal kick to a teammate standing in an offside position in the other half of the field, offside is not called as you cannot be offside on a goal kick.

In the 9,000-plus matches that I have officiated, I have never seen a goal scored directly off a goal kick. But a few times I have seen the goal kick go directly to a player standing in an offside position in the other half of the field and had to briefly explain why offside was not called.

The Corner Kick

Law 17: The Corner Kick

A corner kick is awarded when the whole ball, having last touched a player of the defending team, passes over the goal line either on the ground or in the air and a goal was not scored.

The ball is placed inside or on the line of the 1-yard corner arc on the side of the goal where the ball left the field. The corner flag post is not moved and opponents remain at least 10 yards from the corner arc until the ball is kicked.

A corner kick is another restart in which a player cannot be offside directly from the kick. So players can stand wherever they want on the field, including by the goalkeeper. Watch out for jostling near the keeper. A preventive officiating technique is to whistle a foul if the kick has been taken, or verbally warn if the ball is out of play, as soon as you see pushing or holding by the goal. You should not have any more problems on corner kicks for the rest of the game.

Trick Kick

Some teams will try a bit of a trick play on a corner kick. #11 has the ball and is about to take the kick. She kicks the ball slightly while yelling, "Jill, you take the kick!" #11 runs toward the goal while her teammate goes to the corner and starts dribbling, since the corner kick was already taken when #11 kicked the ball. Be alert for a play like this that is perfectly legal.

Kids Say the Funniest Things

Kids says the darndest things, especially little kids playing soccer. Recently, in refereeing a Boys-Under-9 game, gray was attacking and the ball went off white over the goal line. So I pointed to the corner flag and said, "Corner kick."

A little gray player then said, "For which team?"

Additional Items to Know

Let's go over more items that you should know. These do not fit easily into any given rule.

Blood Is Thicker...

Should an official notice a player bleeding, wait until the ball is out of play and tell the player, captain or coach that the player needs to come off the field. The team can substitute at this point. The player cannot return to the field until the bleeding has stopped, there is no blood on the skin or uniform and the player in question has been checked by an official.

Than Water

During a stoppage in play, water bottles are to be handed to players on the field at the touchline. Water bottles should not be thrown on to the field. Players need to stay on the field during a stoppage in play.

When the Officials Make a Bad Call

If a bad call is made and the referee knows it, the call could be reversed as long as play was not restarted. But do this very infrequently.

Should reversing a decision not be a good option, restart play quickly. The quicker play is restarted, the less time a team has to stew over a bad call. After all, it's very hard for players to argue when the opposing team has put the ball in play and is moving down the field.

On this topic, the officials should admit a mistake when it's painfully obvious to everyone. Such as the (nonhard) foul that was whistled but an advantage situation quickly materialized. Just say, "You had the advantage so I should not have blown the whistle. Take the kick, please."

But you cannot apologize every time a player believes you missed a call as you will be perceived as very wishy-washy and apologizing frequently will undermine your authority.

Assessments

Finally, we come to the role of the assessor, that person who comes to your match to rate your performance and give you helpful ideas. Listen to what the assessor has to say, and it's probably a very good idea to act on the advice as well.

Probably very few of your games will be assessed by a person trained to do so; however, you are being assessed every game by players, coaches and spectators. Listen to criticism that they have of you. If you see **patterns of criticism developing**, act on them.

When I started refereeing, I heard comments like "Ref, let us play," "The teams are playing nicely, so could you call less fouls?" and "You meant well, but you interrupted play too much." I learned to whistle fewer fouls while still maintaining control of the game, to everyone's benefit.

Success

I hope that this book has given you some ideas on how to improve your officiating.

You will know that you have become a good referee when:

• After the game, players and coaches go out of their way to say "Good job," "Great job!" or "You were the best ref we've had all season!"

• People say to you, "Could you officiate all our games?"

• Your phone and e-mail account become hot with more and more assignments.

• You are assigned top games.

• You are asked to officiate tournaments out-of-state and maybe even abroad.

• You receive officiating awards from leagues and referee associations.

This means you have succeeded. Congratulations!

Now you come to an important fork in the road. Or as Yogi Berra has said, "When you come to the fork in the road, take it!"

Some successful referees take the correct road. They know that they have succeeded because of their knowledge of the Laws of the Game and their application, their hustle, their positive attitude, their fairness and firmness plus their approachability. And they continue doing all these great things.

Other successful refs take the wrong road. Their success goes to their head and they somehow think the game is now about them.

I have heard these comments about refs:

- "He used to be really good and now all he wants to do is argue with the coaches."

- "He's a good ref. The problem is, he thinks that he is a great ref and lets everyone know it."

- "She was a very good referee. Now people don't take her seriously as her body has become as big as a house."

- "He was one of our best referees. Now he hardly moves out of the kick-off circle."

Which road are you going to take?

Code of Ethics

Maybe I have a Norman Rockwell-like view of society, but I truly believe in respecting authority figures such as doctors, police officers, firefighters, teachers, clergy and, certainly, referees.

Not everybody shares my view. Too bad many leaders have contributed to this question authority attitude by their very unethical actions. Don't dare let that happen to you as a referee.

The United States Soccer Federation has even created this wonderful Code of Ethics for Referees:

1. That I shall always maintain the utmost respect for the game of soccer.

2. That I will conduct myself honorably at all times and maintain the dignity of my position.

3. That I shall always honor a contractual obligation.

4. That I will endeavor to attend local meetings and clinics so as best to know the Laws of the Game and their proper interpretation.

5. That I will always strive to achieve maximum team work with any fellow referees and assistant referees.

6. That I shall be loyal to my fellow referees and assistant referees, and never knowingly promote criticism of them.

7. That I shall be in good physical condition so as to be in the right place at the right time.

8. That I will control the players effectively by being courteous and considerate without sacrificing firmness.

9. That I shall do my utmost to assist my fellow officials to better themselves and their work.

10. That I shall not make statements about any game except to clarify an interpretation of the Laws of the Game.

11. That I consider it a privilege to be part of the United States Soccer Federation and I will strive to make my actions reflect credit upon that organization and its affiliates.

Glossary

Advantage-A clause in the rules in which the officials allow play to continue rather than stopping for an infraction as doing so would actually benefit the team that committed the infraction. Referee signals advantage by raising both arms from side of body and yelling, "Play on!"

AR-An assistant referee.

Assistant Referee-An official positioned along the touchline who communicates with the referee with a flag signal.

Attacker-Player whose team is in possession of the ball.

Caution-A formal warning by the referee signified by the display of a yellow card.

Charging-Body contact undertaken against an opponent in order to win possession of the ball. If done unfairly, it is a penal foul.

Club Linesman-A person volunteering his or her service on the touchline, in the absence of a qualified assistant referee ,who signals when the ball is over the touchline by raising the flag.

Coach-The team official allowed on or by the bench who gives tactical advice and instruction during the game.

Corner Arc-The one-yard quarter circle in the corner of the field marking where a corner kick is taken.

Corner Flag-The flag in each corner of the field that is not less than five feet high with a non-pointed top.

Corner Kick-The restart of play after the ball passes over the goal line and did not go into the goal after being last touched by a defender.

Crossbar-The horizontal beam that forms the top of a goal and sits on top of the two goal posts; it is 24 feet long and supported 8 feet above the ground.

Defender-A player on the team in which their opponents have possession of the ball.

Diagonal System of Control-The internationally recognized system of game control with one referee and two assistant referees.

Direct Kick-A free kick from which a goal can be scored directly, awarded as a result of a penal foul committed outside the fouling team's penalty area.

Dissent-A form of misconduct consisting of protesting an official's call. It is punishable by a caution.

Dropped Ball-A means of restarting play after a stoppage caused by something other than an infraction by one player.

Free Kick-A kick awarded to a team due to an infraction by the opposing team. The kick is free from interference from opponents.

Goal-1. The structure 8-yards wide and 8-feet tall on the goal line and defended by the respective team. 2. A score occurring when the ball passes entirely over the goal line and into the goal.

Goalkeeper-The player on each team designated as the one entitled to legally handle the ball inside the team's own penalty area. The goalkeeper is required to wear a jersey that is different in color from each team.

Goal Line-The line at the end of the field on which the goals are placed.

Goal Post-A vertical beam that extends eight feet high to form the side of the goal.

Halftime-The intermission between the end of the first half and the start of the second half.

Handling-The deliberate use of the arm or body to play the ball. A penal foul, except when done by the goalkeeper inside the penalty area.

Holding-A penal foul, consisting of unfairly hindering or restraining an opponent, usually by using the arms or hands.

Impeding-Physically impeding or obstructing the progress of an opponent. Also called "obstructing." Penalized by an indirect kick.

Indirect Kick-A free kick that requires the touch of a second player before a goal can be scored, awarded as a result of a non-penal infraction.

Jumps at an Opponent-A penal foul when the jumping is directed at an opponent to prevent that player from making a play on the ball.

Kicks or Attempts to Kick an Opponent-A penal foul consisting of unfair contact against an opponent by using the foot or leg.

Kick-Off-The means of starting the half or restarting the match following a goal. The kick-off takes place from the middle of the kick-off circle.

Kick-Off Circle-The circle marking the 10-yard radius from the place of the kick-off. Also called the center circle.

Misconduct-An unacceptable violation of the rules punishable by a caution or send-off.

Obstructing-See "impeding."

Offside-A player in an advanced position that is illegal either interferes with a play or an opponent or gains an advantage by being in that position.

Out of Play-When the ball goes over the goal line or touchline, either on the ground or in the air. The ball is also out of play when the game has been stopped by the referee.

Penal Foul-One of the 10 fouls resulting in the awarding of either a direct kick or penalty kick.

Penalty Arc-The markings on the field outside the penalty area keeping players 10 yards from the penalty kick, with the exception of the kicker and goalkeeper.

Penalty Area-The 18 x 44-yard area around each goal, within which the defending team's keeper can legally handle the ball and a penal foul by the defensive team is punishable by a penalty kick.

Penalty Kick-A kick from the penalty spot, 12 yards from goal, on which a goal can be scored directly.

Penalty Spot-The marked area 12 yards from the middle of each goal where penalty kicks are taken.

Persistent Infringement-Repeated fouling resulting in a caution.

Pushes an Opponent-A penal foul from the unfair use of the hands or arms to push an opposing player.

Referee-The official in charge of the soccer match.

Restart-Any method of resuming play after a stoppage in play.

Send-Off-A formal ejection by the referee signified by the display of a red card.

Serious Foul Play-Occurs if a player uses excessive force or brutality when challenging for the ball on the field against an opponent when the ball is in play. Punishable by a send-off.

Spits at an Opponent-A penal foul AND sending-off offense.

Strikes or Attempts to Strike an Opponent-Involves any other part of the body except the leg as well as using the ball or any hurled object. A penal foul and generally a send-off offense as well.

Stoppage Time-Time added to the end of the half (or overtime period) to compensate for playing time lost to injuries, substitutions, time-wasting or any other cause that the referee deems appropriate.

Substitute-A player not currently participating in the match.

Throw-In-The method of restarting play after the ball has gone out of bounds over the touchline.

Touchline-The boundary line marking the side of the field.

Trips or Attempts to Trip an Opponent-A penal foul resulting from the impeding or catching of an opponent's foot, or the attempt to do this, so as to knock the opposing player down.

Unsporting Behavior-Unacceptable conduct that is punished by a caution.

Violent Conduct-Occurs when a player or substitute is guilty of aggression towards an opponent when they are not contesting for the ball or towards any other person (a teammate, the referee, an assistant referee, a spectator, etc.). The ball can be in or out of play and the aggression can occur either on or off the field of play.

Index

Made in the USA
San Bernardino, CA
11 December 2014